Longarm's All Fired Up . . .

Longarm lit another match, grabbed one of the bottles, and jammed the flame against the liquor-soaked cloth. It caught instantly, flaring up in blue fire. Knowing he had only seconds to act, Longarm sprang into the street and flung the bottle as hard as he could at the open door. It sailed through even as the men holed up in the shop opened fire on him. He threw himself toward an alley as bullets whipped past his head.

Somebody inside yelled, and then the bottle exploded. Longarm heard the blast, followed by a man's scream. He struck another match, lit the fuse on the second bomb, and rolled into the street. Bullets whined through the air above him as he pitched the bottle underhanded into the shop. Then he launched into another desperate roll, this time away from the searching lead.

The second bottle exploded in a ball of fire when it had barely cleared the doorway, sending splinters of glass spraying through the shop. Longarm lay on his belly, his whole body covered now with a thick coating of sand, and waited to see what was going to happen...

TABOR EVANS

LONGARM

AND THE
SAND PIRATES

JOVE BOOKS, NEW YORK

THE BERKLEY PUBLISHING GROUP
Published by the Penguin Group
Penguin Group (USA) Inc.
375 Hudson Street, New York, New York 10014, USA

Penguin Group (Canada), 90 Eglinton Avenue East, Suite 700, Toronto, Ontario M4P 2Y3, Canada
(a division of Pearson Penguin Canada Inc.)
Penguin Books Ltd., 80 Strand, London WC2R 0RL, England
Penguin Group Ireland, 25 St. Stephen's Green, Dublin 2, Ireland (a division of Penguin Books Ltd.)
Penguin Group (Australia), 250 Camberwell Road, Camberwell, Victoria 3124, Australia
(a division of Pearson Australia Group Pty. Ltd.)
Penguin Books India Pvt. Ltd., 11 Community Centre, Panchsheel Park, New Delhi—110 017, India
Penguin Group (NZ), 67 Apollo Drive, Rosedale, North Shore 0632, New Zealand
(a division of Pearson New Zealand Ltd.)
Penguin Books (South Africa) (Pty.) Ltd., 24 Sturdee Avenue, Rosebank, Johannesburg 2196,
South Africa

Penguin Books Ltd., Registered Offices: 80 Strand, London WC2R 0RL, England

This is a work of fiction. Names, characters, places, and incidents either are the product of the author's imagination or are used fictitiously, and any resemblance to actual persons, living or dead, business establishments, events, or locales is entirely coincidental.

LONGARM AND THE SAND PIRATES

A Jove Book / published by arrangement with the author

PRINTING HISTORY
Jove edition / January 2010

Copyright © 2009 by Penguin Group (USA) Inc.
Cover illustration by Miro Sinovcic.

ISBN: 978-0-515-14742-1

JOVE®
Jove Books are published by The Berkley Publishing Group,
a division of Penguin Group (USA) Inc.,
375 Hudson Street, New York, New York 10014.
JOVE® is a registered trademark of Penguin Group (USA) Inc.
The "J" design is a trademark of Penguin Group (USA) Inc.

PRINTED IN THE UNITED STATES OF AMERICA

10 9 8 7 6 5 4 3 2 1

Chapter 1

There might not be any flames out there, thought Longarm as he stared across the vast, sandy wasteland, or any
devils with cloven hooves, barbed tails, and pitchforks . . .
but it was still Hell. Even here on the edge, with some
low, cool gray mountains behind him, he could feel the
heat coming off the desert.

The town that had planted itself in the relatively nar-
row, grassy strip between the barren mountains and the
equally barren desert was called Brimstone. The name
was appropriate since the settlement was on the edge of
Hades, Longarm decided.

"There's nothing out there for you, my son."

Longarm looked around to see who had come up behind him. A thin-faced, gray-haired priest in a brown robe
stood there. His friendly features wore a gentle smile.

"No offense, padre," said Longarm, "but how do you
know what I'm looking for?"

The priest shook his head. "It doesn't matter. There's
nothing out there for anyone, no matter what they're looking for. Nothing but death."

"Some folks look for that their whole lives," Longarm muttered.

The priest heard him and nodded. "Indeed they do. But you don't strike me as one of them. You look like the sort of man who embraces life, instead of running from it."

Longarm couldn't help but grin. "I ain't much on running from anything."

He had never needed to run from much in his life, at least not since the Late Unpleasantness had finally ground to a halt and he had headed out into the world from West-by-God-Virginia, a gangling youth fresh from seeing the elephant. After eating what seemed like a ton of trail dust pushing cows up from Texas to the railheads in Kansas, he had drifted into the law—enforcing it, not practicing it. For a goodly number of years, he'd been carrying a badge for Uncle Sam as a deputy United States marshal, although nobody in Brimstone was aware of that. He had ridden in a short time earlier, looking like any other chuck-line rider.

Longarm's tall, rangy form was clad in a faded work shirt, denim trousers, and black stovepipe boots. A flat-crowned, snuff-brown Stetson sat on his head at a slightly rakish angle. His high-cheekboned face, which led some people to believe he had Indian blood, was permanently tanned to the color of old saddle leather. The curling longhorn mustaches that adorned his upper lip were the same mahogany shade as his hair. A Colt .45 Peacemaker with well-worn walnut grips rode butt-forward in a cross-draw rig on his left hip. He looked like the cowboy he had once been, and that's the way he wanted to keep it, for now anyway.

It wouldn't do any good for the citizens of Brimstone to know that he was a lawman on the trail of as vicious a gang of owlhoots as he had tracked recently.

Now the priest went on, "What brings you to Brimstone, my son?"

"Just drifting, padre. Got no particular place to be, and I'm taking my time about getting there."

The priest frowned slightly. "The scriptures say that pride goeth before a fall, but I'm not certain that a complete lack of ambition is a good thing, either."

"Oh, I've got some ambition, Father," Longarm said with a grin. "My ambition right now is to go into that saloon over yonder and wet my whistle."

The priest chuckled. "I'm a good Irishman as well as a servant of the Lord, so I can't very well condemn you for something I've been known to do myself."

"Want to join me?" Longarm asked as he tilted his head toward the Ace High Saloon.

"I'd better not. I need to get back down to the mission. You should be careful in there, though. That can be a rough place." A soft laugh came from the padre. "I forgot . . . You're not the sort of man who runs away from trouble."

"Probably be smarter if I was," said Longarm. "And I'd damn sure—I mean darned sure—have fewer scars."

He lifted a hand in farewell and ambled toward the saloon, past the hitch rail where he had tied the army remount he had picked up at Fort Stockton. The McClellan saddle was the one thing about his outfit that didn't say cowhand, but it was what he was used to, he liked it, and so that's what he rode.

He asked himself what the chances were that he'd walk into the saloon and see Colonel Garth. That wasn't a rank; it was the man's name. He was the leader of the gang of outlaws Longarm had chased halfway across Texas, and after barely missing Garth several times, the big lawman figured he wouldn't be lucky enough to stumble over him now.

But sometimes miracles happened, because as Longarm pushed the batwings aside and stepped into the saloon's shadowy interior, he spotted Garth's burly figure hunched at the bar. The man was almost as tall as Longarm, with a barrel chest, massive shoulders, and a bushy black beard. He wore buckskins and a wide-brimmed hat with a round crown, the type of outfit that the old mountain men some-times wore. His hand was so big the beer mug he picked up in it looked a little odd, sort of like a toy.

Garth was the only one of the gang Longarm knew by sight, because his boss up in Denver, Chief Marshal Billy Vail, had had a reward dodger with a drawing of Garth on it. Vail had let Longarm study that picture when he handed out the assignment to chase down Garth and his gang.

So Longarm didn't know how many of the other men in the saloon might be part of Garth's bunch. Maybe none of them, maybe half a dozen or more. Even though a part of him wanted to draw his gun, wallop Garth over the head with it, and drag him down to the local jail, he couldn't risk making such a move until he had a better lay of the land.

So he bellied up to the bar not far from the outlaw, gave him a pleasant nod, and said to the bartender, "You wouldn't happen to have any Maryland rye back there, would you, old son?"

The bartender, a middle-aged, balding man who had the world-weary look of bartenders everywhere, asked, "Tom Moore all right?"

Longarm grinned. "Nothing would be better right now. Give me a shot with a beer chaser."

What were the odds he would run across a saloon that

stocked his favorite liquor out here on the ass end of nowhere? About the same as the odds that he would walk in and find the fugitive he was after standing right beside him, he supposed.

As far as he knew, Garth had never gotten a look at him and might not even know that a federal lawman was after him. So when the bartender set the glass of Maryland rye in front of him, Longarm picked it up, turned to Garth, and said, "Here's to your health, old son."

Garth grunted in surprise at being addressed, lifted his mug, and gave Longarm a civil nod. "Yeah, thanks. Yours, too."

They drank. Longarm said, "Ah," and wiped the back of his other hand across his mouth. Then he lifted his beer, took a sip, and said, apparently making casual conversation, "You from around these parts, mister?"

Garth shook his bull-like head. "No, just passin' through."

"On the way to where?" Longarm asked with a chuckle. "There ain't nothing out here to speak of."

Garth didn't seem suspicious at all. "Figured to work my way on west to El Paso."

Longarm frowned. "I'm not from around here, either, but I didn't think there was anything for a hundred miles west of here except desert. You'd have to circle around all that sand to get to El Paso, wouldn't you?"

"No. There's an old wagon road through there. That's what I've been told, anyway."

Longarm hadn't heard about that. Did Garth really intend to lead his gang across the desert, or was he just bullshitting?

Sounding doubtful, Longarm said, "I don't reckon I'd want to start out across there, especially by myself."

"I never said I was by myself. I got some partners travelin' with me. We'll take plenty of water with us and be all right."

"Better you than me," said Longarm. "Where are these partners of yours?"

Garth finally frowned a little. "Say, you sure do like to ask questions, don't you?"

Longarm held up his hands, palms out, and grinned. "Sorry," he said. "I've always been a mite too talkative. It's one of my failings. So's a fondness for poker." He pointed with a thumb toward a table in the back of the room. "Looks like those fellas have got a game going. Want to see if we can sit in on it?"

He knew from things he had heard and read about Colonel Garth that the man couldn't resist the lure of the pasteboards. Garth hesitated, then said, "Yeah, I wouldn't mind playin' a few hands."

Longarm picked up his beer, which he had barely touched, and ambled over to the table where the game was going on. Garth got the bartender to refill his beer and followed. A hand was just ending, and one of the players shoved back his chair and stood up.

"I'm cleaned out, boys," he announced. "Sorry."

Longarm said, "How about we bring some new money to the table?"

The remaining players nodded and muttered agreement. Longarm and Garth sat down. There were four other players in the game—a couple of townsmen and two men who looked like ranchers. There were cattle spreads scattered north and south of Brimstone, Longarm recalled.

Longarm didn't care whether he won or lost the game. He was playing strictly to study Garth and the other men in the saloon. Garth hadn't paid any attention to any of them, and none of them had glanced in his direction. Longarm had a hunch that none of the rest of Garth's gang was in here. He had to be careful anyway. Even if he took Garth prisoner, word would get around town and the rest of the gang would come after him. It would be better if he could pick them off one at a time without anyone else knowing, starting with the leader.

By the time Garth had had enough of the poker game, night had fallen. He threw in his cards at the end of a hand and said, "I think I'm gonna go get something to eat."

"Sounds good to me," Longarm agreed. "I noticed a hash house across the street."

One of the townies said, "The food's good there, boys."

"We'll give it a try," Longarm said as he pushed his chair back. Garth went along with him without any argument.

The outlaw paused, however, as they stepped out onto the boardwalk. "I didn't get your name, friend," he said.

"It's Parker," Longarm said. "Custis Parker."

Parker actually was his middle name—he'd been dubbed Custis Parker Long when he was born—and he used it from time to time as an alias. Too many people were aware that Custis Long was actually a federal lawman, better known to friends and enemies alike as Longarm.

"Glad to make your acquaintance, Parker. I'm Colonel Garth."

Longarm raised his eyebrows in surprise, as most men would on hearing that name. "Colonel? You in the army?"

Garth laughed. "Not hardly. That's really my name. My pa called me that after an officer he served with durin' the Mexican War. Colonel Thaddeus Henshaw Garth. It's a mouthful, ain't it?"

"Yeah, but I reckon it suits you."

"You wouldn't happen to be lookin' for work, would you, Parker?"

"Well, that would depend on the job," Longarm replied carefully. Was Garth about to ask him to join the gang? Stranger things had happened, he supposed. They had hit it off well, and Longarm had the look of a tough hombre who might be a good addition to the gang.

"I lost one of my partners in San Antonio about a week ago," Garth said.

That would be the fella who'd been shot down while Garth and his men were robbing a bank in San Antonio, thought Longarm. He had reached the city the next day after the robbery.

"I didn't figure on replacin' him until we got to El Paso," Garth went on, "but since good fortune seems to have thrown us together, I didn't think it would hurt anything to ask."

"I appreciate that. You probably ought to know, though, that I, uh, ain't exactly on what you'd call the right side of the law."

Garth threw back his head and guffawed. "Well, hell, Custis, neither am I!" He clapped a hand on Longarm's back so hard that it almost staggered the big lawman. "Come on, let's get somethin' to eat, and then I'll introduce you to the rest of the boys and see what they think."

"Sounds good to me," said Longarm. This way he could get a good look at the rest of the outlaws, so he'd know who he was after.

The food at the hash house was good, just like the townie had said. Longarm enjoyed the meal. Garth really wasn't a bad sort, as murdering, stealing assholes who deserved to be behind bars or dancing at the end of a hang-rope went.

When they were finished, Garth led Longarm outside. "The rest of the bunch is down the street at the whorehouse. We'll go find 'em."

"Whorehouse, eh? I'm surprised you weren't there, too."

Garth smirked. "I had to let the gals rest up a mite. I wear 'em out faster than regular fellas do."

Longarm didn't know how much truth there was to that boastful claim and didn't care. He went up the street with Garth to a two-story adobe house that was one of the largest and most impressive buildings in Brimstone. The place probably did a booming business from the cowboys who worked on the nearby ranches.

Garth pounded on the door. The man who opened it was short and scrawny, with a soup-strainer mustache that looked like it might weigh more than he did. There was nothing puny about the double-barreled sawed-off he held, though.

"Oh, it's you, Colonel," the man said as he recognized Garth. He lowered the scattergun. "Who's your friend?"

"Fella name of Parker who may be ridin' with us," Garth explained. "Parker, this is Iron Mike Dumont."

Longarm nodded and howdied, then said, "No offense, Dumont, but you don't look like the sort of hombre they'd call Iron Mike."

"The whores give me that name," Dumont said, preening like a peacock, "on account of how hard my pecker gets and how it stays that way even after I'm done with 'em." He reached for his trouser buttons. "I can show you—"

"No, that's all right," Longarm said quickly. "I'd be mighty happy to take your word for it."

Garth laughed. "Ol' Iron Mike's right proud of his pecker. He'll show it to just about anybody."

"That's true," Dumont said with a solemn nod. He stepped aside and gestured with the sawed-off. "Come on in. Thinkin' about joinin' up with us, are you, Parker?"

"Colonel here asked me after we'd been playing some poker at the saloon," Longarm explained.

Dumont nodded as he closed the door behind them. "Yeah, that's how he likes to size a fella up. Colonel says he can tell more about a man by the way he plays cards than any other way."

The three of them went from the foyer into a parlor where a heavyset Mexican woman in a red silk dress was sitting in the middle of a brocaded divan. She was flanked by two soiled doves in skimpy shifts, one at each end of the divan. To the madam's right was a slender blonde whose fair hair hung most of the way down her back. On her left was a scared-looking black girl who probably wasn't more than fifteen years old. Longarm's jaw started to tighten in anger when he saw her, but he suppressed the reaction. A would-be desperado like the man he was pretending to be wouldn't give a damn how young or how scared the girl was.

"*Hola, Señor Colonel,*" the woman said. "These two are the only girls I have available right now. All the others are upstairs with your men. But I'm sure they would be glad to accommodate you and your friend."

Garth grinned over at Longarm. "What do you say, Parker? You want the little darkie, or should I take her?"

"I'll take her," Longarm said without hesitation. He knew that if he balked, she'd wind up going upstairs with Garth instead.

"Like that dark meat, eh?" Garth grinned at the blonde. "Come on, honey, I'll give you a ride you won't forget anytime soon."

The madam had to practically push the younger girl off the divan. Longarm took hold of her arm. "Don't worry," he told her. "It'll be all right." He felt her trembling a little under his touch.

"I'll wait down here," Dumont called after them as they started up the stairs. "Even ol' Iron Mike's gotta recuperate ever' now and then."

When they reached the upstairs corridor, which was dimly lit by candles stuck in holders in the wall, Garth lifted a hand in farewell. "See you in a little while, Parker," he said. "We'll all get together downstairs and have a drink. You can get to know the rest of the bunch."

"Sounds good," Longarm agreed. He followed the girl to one of the doors that lined the corridor. It stood slightly open, to indicate that the room wasn't in use. The two of them went inside. The girl used the light from the corridor to guide her as she struck a match and lit a small lamp on a side table. Then she closed the door, reached down to the hem of her shift, and peeled the garment up and over her head. She wasn't wearing anything under it.

"Honey, you put that back on," Longarm told her.

She stood there holding the shift so that it hid some of her body. Longarm thought that was instinctive on her part, not artifice. She gave him a puzzled frown as she said in a soft voice, "You don't wanna lay with me, mister?"

"It ain't a matter of want to, it's a matter of gonna, and I ain't," said Longarm. "What I'm gonna do is look away for a minute, and when I turn back around, I want you to be wearing that thing. It ain't much, but it's better than nothing."

She looked completely confused, but when Longarm turned back to her a moment later, she was wearing the shift again. "You one strange cowboy, mister," she told him. "If you didn't like me, why'd you pick me to bring up here?"

"I never said I don't like you. It's just that you shouldn't be doing this."

She sighed. "Oh, Lordy. You ain't one o' them gentlemen who thump the Bible all week long and then come fuck a whore on Saturday night, is you?"

"It ain't Saturday, and I always figured the Good Book was meant for reading, not thumping. I know the difference between right and wrong, though, and you don't need to be doing this."

She shrugged. "Girl's got to eat, whether she likes what's she's doin' to earn her livin' or not."

"What's your name?"

"Coralie."

Longarm took a double eagle from his pocket and pressed it into her hand. She stared at it and then at him, as startled as if he had just handed her a baby giraffe.

"Listen to me, Coralie," Longarm said quietly. "You hide that gold piece and don't let anybody know you've got it. Not any of the other girls, and damn sure not that *mamacita* downstairs. I happen to know there's a stagecoach that comes down here from Fort Stockton. It'll be here in three days. When that day comes, you slip out, buy yourself a decent dress, and take that coach to the fort."

Coralie shook her head. "They ain't gonna let no colored girl ride that stagecoach."

"Yeah, they will, because you'll have money, and they'll like the color of it. When you get to the fort, find the quartermaster. He's a man named Duffy. Tell him that Custis sent you and said for him to find you a job. At first, it may not be anything better than doing laundry . . . but that's better than what you're doing here."

She blinked rapidly, and he thought he saw the glint of tears in her eyes. "You really mean all this shit you're tellin' me, mister?"

"I damned sure do," said Longarm. "You do like I tell you, and you won't ever have to come back here."

"You . . . you don't even know me. Don't know the things I've done or how I got here."

"I don't have to know. Now, will you do like I said?"

Her hand clenched tightly around the double eagle. "Yeah," she whispered. "Yeah, I will." She looked up at him, and then she reached for the buttons of his trousers. "I got to do somethin' to pay you back."

Longarm caught hold of her wrist and stopped her. "No, you don't."

"Then, to thank you . . ."

He shook his head. "Just get out of here when you get the chance and make a better life for yourself. That'll be thanks enough for me."

"Well . . . all right." She laughed. "But like I said, mister, you one strange cowboy."

He took a three-for-a-nickel cheroot from his shirt pocket and clenched it between his teeth. "I been called worse," he told her with a grin.

Chapter 2

Longarm waited until a suitable time had passed, then went downstairs, leaving Coralie in the upstairs room. When he stepped into the parlor, he saw a couple of men standing at a bar with Iron Mike Dumont, tossing back drinks. The madam and the rest of the whores were nowhere in sight. Dumont waved Longarm over.

"Hey, Parker, come say howdy to a couple more o' the boys. This here is Ed Glennister and Charley Hargrove."

Longarm nodded to Glennister, who was a tall, skinny, gray-faced man, and Hargrove, who was short and stocky, with the red, bulbous nose of a heavy drinker.

"Colonel's talkin' to Parker here about ridin' with us," Dumont went on.

"Is that so?" Glennister said. "I don't know that I cotton much to the idea of invitin' a fella in without gettin' to know him first."

"That's why I'm here, I reckon," said Longarm. He gestured toward the bar. "Pour me a drink, would you, Iron Mike?" He tossed back the whiskey Dumont handed him, then said to Glennister, "Anything you want to know about me, mister, ask away. My life's an open book."

"Where are you from?"

"West-by-God-Virginia." Always better to be truthful about the simple questions.

"Fight in the war?"

"I did, but don't ask me for which side. I sort of disremember."

That brought a chuckle from Hargrove. "That was twenty years ago," he said. "I don't reckon it really matters now."

"No, I suppose not," Glennister said, although his tone was a little surly. Bluntly, he asked, "Done time?"

"Yuma," Longarm said. That was sort of true. He had been to Yuma Territorial Prison out in Arizona on numerous occasions. He had even pretended to be a prisoner there once, to carry out an assignment for Billy Vail.

Hargrove said, "From what I hear, Yuma's a rough place."

"It ain't a picnic, that's for damned sure."

"Know anybody we might know?" Glennister persisted.

"How about Big John Barbour?" Longarm said, naming an outlaw who'd been dead for a couple of years.

"He and his bunch got shot up pretty bad at Santa Fe a while back, didn't they?" Dumont asked.

"Yeah."

"Barbour was killed, if I recollect right, along with the rest of his men except for a couple who got away."

Longarm touched his side. "I can show you the scar I picked up that day."

Again, what he was saying wasn't that far from the truth. He had been in Santa Fe the day Big John Barbour had been killed in a shoot-out. In fact, he was the one who'd ventilated the ugly son of a bitch, and the scar on his side was where one of Barbour's slugs had creased him during the fracas.

Hargrove said, "You sound like you're a man who'll do to ride the river with, Parker."

"Yeah, I reckon," Glennister admitted.

Footsteps clumped on the stairs. Longarm glanced around and saw Colonel Garth descending along with two more men. Garth grinned when he spotted Longarm and said, "Well, the whole bunch is here. You met Ed and Charley?"

"Yeah, we been talking," Longarm said.

Garth jerked a thumb at his companions as they reached the bottom of the stairs. "This is Paco Malone and Hair-Trigger Thompson."

Longarm barely had time to recognize the third man's name before Thompson stepped around Garth, looked at him, and exclaimed, "Shit! That's a lawman!"

Well, if that didn't beat all. The final member of Garth's gang had to be a low-down, no-account skunk Longarm had arrested a few years earlier as part of a counterfeiting scheme. A lot of the men Longarm went after in his job wound up dead, either from a bullet or a noose, and the ones who went to prison, like Thompson, usually stayed there for a good long time. Either Thompson had gotten a light sentence for his part in the scheme, or else he had broken out before serving all his time. It didn't matter which, of course. At the moment, the only important thing was that Longarm found himself in the middle of six cold-blooded killers who were suddenly clawing at the guns on their hips.

His only hope was to move as fast as he had ever moved in his long, adventurous career. He still had the empty whiskey glass in his left hand. His arm shot out. He smashed the glass in the middle of Iron Mike Dumont's face, pulping the little man's prominent nose and shattering the glass so that blood spurted from the cuts it left on Dumont's cheeks.

At the same time, his right hand flashed across to the Colt in the cross-draw rig. The revolver appeared in his fingers as if by magic and spouted fire and lead less than a shaved heartbeat later. His first shot was aimed at Colonel Garth, who was supposed to be the best gunhand in the gang. Garth was already moving as Longarm squeezed the trigger, though, so the bullet shattered Garth's upper left arm instead of plowing into his heart as Longarm had intended. The slug's impact was enough to knock Garth halfway around and drop him to one knee, though, putting him out of the fight for the moment.

Longarm grabbed Dumont, who was screaming in pain from his broken nose and lacerated face, and bulled to his right, dragging the little outlaw with him. He collided with Charley Hargrove and knocked the stocky outlaw down. At the same time, Longarm snapped a shot at Paco Malone and saw blood spurt from the half-breed outlaw's head.

Ed Glennister had his gun out and started blazing away at Longarm, but the big lawman had pulled Dumont between him and Glennister. One of Glennister's bullets nicked Dumont's arm and made him yell that much louder. Longarm thrust his Colt under Dumont's arm and fired at Glennister. The outlaw's head jerked back as a black-rimmed hole appeared in his forehead. Blood began to well out of the hole as he collapsed.

Garth was back on his feet, swinging his gun up, and Hair-Trigger Thompson hadn't been touched yet. Longarm slung Dumont at them like a rag doll. Dumont crashed into them, keeping them from firing for a few seconds.

Hargrove grabbed Longarm's legs, trying to bring him down. Longarm slashed downward with the heavy revolver. The barrel raked across the side of Hargrove's head, stunning him and opening up a gash. Longarm pulled out of his grip and stumbled a couple of steps across the parlor. Garth and Thompson were about to open fire on him again.

Before they could pull their triggers, something came sailing down from the second-floor landing and shattered. Flames leaped up like living things between Longarm and the two outlaws. He realized that someone had thrown a lamp from up there to distract Garth and Thompson. He squeezed off a couple of shots, but from the way the owlhoots scrambled out the front door of the whorehouse, he knew he hadn't hit them. They must have decided to take off for the tall and uncut rather than stay and continue the battle.

Dumont stopped yelling long enough to crawl after them. Longarm tried to make it through the fire and nab the little outlaw, but the heat was too great and forced him back. That left Malone and Glennister, both of whom appeared to be dead, and Hargrove, who regained his senses long enough to pick up his gun and spray bullets wildly around the room from where he lay on the floor. Longarm felt the hot kiss of a slug passing close by his cheek without touching it as he spun around and kicked Hargrove in the jaw as hard as he could. Hargrove went over backward, flinging his arms wide.

Screeching, the madam rushed into the parlor and began beating at the flames with a blanket she had brought with her. Several soiled doves, a couple of them stark naked, tried to help put out the fire, too. One of them found a bucket of water somewhere and threw it over the flames. Longarm grabbed the blanket from the madam and beat out the last of the conflagration, which had burned up most of the parlor rug and scorched the divan and several chairs. Luckily, the flames hadn't reached the bar, or the liquor would have gone up and they never would have gotten the fire out until the place was gutted.

Longarm dropped the blanket and quickly thumbed fresh cartridges into the Peacemaker's cylinder. He snapped it shut and went to check on the three outlaws. Malone and Glennister were dead, all right, both from head wounds, and Charley Hargrove had crossed the divide as well. From the odd angle at which Hargrove's head sat on his shoulders, Longarm knew that his kick had broken the outlaw's neck.

Garth, Thompson, and Dumont were gone, though. He hurried out of the smoky building and heard the swift rataplan of drumming hoofbeats fading into the night. Several townspeople stood around, staring at the whorehouse because it must have sounded like a small war was being fought in there. At the sight of the gun in Longarm's hand, they started backing away.

"Hold it!" he snapped. "Don't worry, I'm a lawman. Those three fellas who came running out of there, where did they go?"

"Are you really a lawman?" one of the townies asked.

"I'd show you my badge and bona fides, but I ain't in the mood," Longarm grated. "Where'd they go?"

Another man said, "They grabbed horses and took off west, toward the desert, mister. They're horse thieves."

"They're worse than that," said Longarm. "They're

wanted for murder and robbery in half a dozen states and territories. You got any local law hereabouts?"

"A town marshal," one of the bystanders replied.

"Somebody fetch him, if he ain't on the way already."

After giving the order, Longarm turned and went back into the house. He had a pretty good idea it was Coralie who had tossed that lamp down and kept him from getting ventilated by Garth and Thompson, and he wanted to thank her before he took off on the trail of the three remaining members of the gang.

The madam started yelling at him in Spanish as soon as he came in. He ignored her and took the stairs two at a time. When he reached the top, he stopped short. His jaw clenched, and he said, "Aw, hell."

Coralie sat with her back against the wall, her smooth brown legs stretched out in front of her. Her eyes were open and she was breathing raggedly, but the crimson stain on her shift was spreading out from under her hands where she had them pressed to her midsection.

She looked up at Longarm, blinked, and said, "Mr. Custis, I . . . I best be givin' you . . . your double eagle . . . back . . . Don't think I'm gonna . . . get to use it . . ."

Longarm knelt beside her. "Don't you say that, honey," he told her. "You're gonna be just fine—"

"I . . . know better . . . I seen men . . . shot like this . . . before . . . It sure . . . hurts . . ."

"I know it does." Longarm leaned closer to her, slipped an arm around her shoulders, cradled her against him. It was all he could do for her now.

One of those wild shots Hargrove had thrown around must have hit her, he thought. That was the only explanation that made any sense. He was glad now he had broken the son of a bitch's neck. He would have traded that, though, for Coralie being all right.

"You're the only man . . . ever been nice to me," she whispered. "Glad I . . . met you . . . Custis."

He felt a little shiver go through her, and then her breath came out of her in a long, soft sigh of finality.

"If you hadn't met me, honey, you'd still be alive," he told her, but she couldn't hear him anymore.

Spanish curses started raining down on him. He looked over and saw that the madam had followed him to the top of the stairs. She stood at the landing, screeching at him because one of her girls was dead and couldn't earn any more money for her.

Carefully, Longarm leaned Coralie against the wall and stood up. The madam fell into a frightened silence at the look on his face as he approached her.

"I want that girl laid to rest proper, with a decent marker, *comprende*? I'll pay for it, and if it ain't done right, I'll know it when I ride back through here, and I'll be coming to see you. You understand me?"

The madam nodded emphatically, making her double chins wobble.

Longarm pushed past her and went down the stairs. As he reached the bottom, a man carrying a shotgun hurried in the front door. Lamplight glinted on the badge pinned to his vest.

"Hold it right there, mister!" he said as he raised the Greener. "What the hell's going on here? Did you kill these men?"

"I damn sure did," said Longarm. "I'd be obliged if you'd lower that shotgun, old son. I don't want your finger getting itchy on the trigger."

"Why the hell should I care what you want?" demanded the local star packer. He was a lean, middle-aged man with a stern face and a salt-and-pepper mustache.

"Because I'm a deputy United States marshal, and these three dead hombres were members of the Colonel Garth gang."

The lawman blinked at him. "You sure about that?"

"Mighty sure. Ask the *mamacita* if you don't believe me. She knows who they were."

"You got any identification?"

"Not on me. It's hidden in a special pocket on my saddle."

"You'll have to fetch it and show it to me."

Longarm reined in the surge of impatient anger that welled up inside him. With every minute that went by, Garth, Thompson, and Dumont were getting farther away from him.

Still, Billy Vail insisted that his deputies cooperate with the local law whenever they could, so Longarm sighed and said, "All right. You might want to send word for the undertaker to come and pick up these bodies."

"Don't tell me how to do my job," the man snapped. "I've been the marshal of Brimstone for a long time."

Longarm and the town marshal left the whorehouse. The man wasn't pointing the Greener at Longarm anymore, but he held it so that he could do so again in a hurry if he needed to. Longarm walked up the street to the hitch rail where he had left his horse, and in a matter of seconds, he had retrieved the little leather folder that held his badge and identification papers. The marshal studied Longarm's bona fides in the light that came through the window of a nearby building, then grunted and handed the folder back.

"Looks like you're who you say you are," the man said. "Now, what in blazes were you doing shooting up my town?"

For the next few minutes, Longarm quickly filled the marshal in on what had happened. He told the man the same thing he had told the madam about wanting a decent burial for Coralie. The marshal scratched his jaw and said, "I'm not sure we can get the padre to go along with that."

"I talked to him earlier. He seemed like a reasonable man, the sort who understands that everybody makes mistakes in their lives. I reckon you can bring him around."

"You'd better talk to him yourself."

Longarm shook his head. "Sorry, Marshal, I ain't got the time. I have to go after those three owlhoots who got away. Since you said you'd been around these parts for a long time, maybe you can answer a question for me."

"I'll try."

"Garth said something about an old wagon road leading through the desert. Any truth to that?"

The local lawman nodded. "Yeah, but that old road's been covered up with sand for years. The dunes shift when the wind blows, you know. Fella name of O'Sullivan got the idea of putting a road through to the other side of the desert for the wagon trains that used to come through these parts. He figured they'd use it because it would cut at least a week off the trip west for them."

"Did he try to make a toll road out of it?" asked Longarm, interested in the story despite the pressing need to get started after the outlaws. The more he knew about where he was going, the better.

The marshal shook his head. "No, he didn't charge for using the road. He built a town smack-dab in the middle of the desert instead."

Longarm's eyebrows rose in surprise. "A town in the middle of a desert? I never heard of such a thing."

"Well, you see, O'Sullivan had heard that there were some springs out there, if you knew where they were and didn't mind digging for them. He hunted for them, found them, and put in a well. Since he had a supply of fresh water, he ran the wagon road right past it and built a trading post there."

"And he charged high for the water and the other supplies he carried," Longarm guessed.

"You've got it. Figured he'd make a fortune doing that. He did all right for a while, well enough that he built a saloon and a whorehouse to go along with the trading post. A few other folks moved in and started businesses of their own. Might've been a nice little town there someday if they could have kept the well going."

"But it dried up?"

"Not really," the marshal said. "They just couldn't keep the sand out of it. O'Sullivan had to dig it out again all the time. Same with the road. A good stiff wind would come along and blow for two or three days, and it was like the road had never been there. O'Sullivan and the men who worked for him had their work cut out for them, just keeping it clear enough for the wagon trains to get through. After a year or so, they gave up. Just rode off and abandoned the place, let the desert have it. No more Abaddon."

"Abaddon?" repeated Longarm with a puzzled frown. The name was vaguely familiar to him, but he couldn't place where he had heard it.

The marshal chuckled humorlessly. "That's another name for Hell, according to some folks. The realm of the dead. I guess O'Sullivan figured it fit, since his town was in the middle of that burning desert, so that's what he called the place."

Longarm remembered the thoughts that had gone through his brain earlier as he stood at the edge of the settlement looking out at the desert. Yeah, it made sense that if somebody was going to put a town out there, they ought to name it after Hell itself.

"You really think those outlaws are going to try to make it through on that old wagon road?" the marshal went on.

"That's what Garth said. I don't know how he came to know about it, but he seemed pretty sure he could follow it. He planned for them to take water with them, though, and they didn't get a chance to do that."

The marshal shook his head. "They'll never make it through without water. The desert's too wide, too hot."

"But if they could find that town and that old well . . ."

"Hell, it's probably completely covered with sand now!"

"But that would be their only chance," Longarm insisted, "and they didn't hesitate to ride out once they found out I was a lawman. He's bound to know something about it." Longarm tugged at his right earlobe as he frowned in thought, then ran his thumbnail along the line of his jaw. "Can you show me where that old road started?"

"Sure," the marshal replied. "You can still see the end of it running from the edge of the desert to Brimstone. O'Sullivan and his men did a good job of plowing and grading it, starting out. They were just fighting a losing battle against the sand."

"I'm gonna gather up some supplies and fill my can-

teens," said Longarm. "Can you meet me back here in
fifteen minutes?"

"You're going after them tonight?" asked the local lawman in surprise.

Longarm nodded. "It's best to travel through the desert
at night, when the sun's down."

"Well, I can't argue with that."

"And there'll be enough moonlight that I ought to be
able to see the tracks their horses left."

"For a while, anyway," the marshal said. "Until the
wind and the sand cover them up."

Longarm gave the man a curt nod and strode toward
the general store, which was still open. He went inside
and bought enough provisions to last for several days,
along with a couple of boxes of ammunition. The .45
rounds would fit both his Colt and the Winchester he always carried. He picked up a couple of extra canteens
while he was at it, too, to go with the two he already
owned. He would have to be careful with the water while
he was in the desert, but he thought that would be enough
to keep him and his horse going.

As he stepped out of the store with a canvas bag full of
the supplies slung over his shoulder, someone came toward
him out of the shadows. He stopped short, his hand tensing
as he readied for a draw, but then he relaxed as he saw that
it wasn't some hard case or outlaw approaching him.

As a matter of fact, it was a very attractive woman with
a slender but nicely curved body and dark brown hair that
fell around her shoulders and framed a pretty face. She
held out a hand toward him and said, "Excuse me, are you
Marshal Long?"

He didn't know how she had heard about him or what

she wanted, but he didn't really have time right now to stand around palavering. He said, "That's right, ma'am, but you'll have to excuse me—"

"I need to talk to you, Marshal." He was about to brush past her when she added, "It's about . . . Abaddon."

Chapter 3

Longarm stopped and looked more closely at her. She was young, somewhere in her early twenties, he judged. He wasn't sure what she could possibly know about some old town in the desert that had been abandoned for years.

Whatever she knew, though, it might come in handy if he knew it, too, so he said, "All right, ma'am, I can give you a minute. What is it you want to tell me?"

"Actually, I have a question for you. I overheard you talking to Marshal Hogan. Is it true that you're going into the desert after some outlaws?"

"Yes, ma'am, it is," Longarm told her with a nod.

She reached out and put her hand on his arm this time. "Then could you take me with you?"

That was about the last thing he would have expected some pretty young gal to ask him in these circumstances. With a frown, he said, "You want to go with me, chasing outlaws into the desert?"

"Well, I don't really care about the outlaws. But I have to find Abaddon. You see, my grandfather was William O'Sullivan."

Longarm shook his head. "No, ma'am, I don't see at all. I don't care who your grandfather was. I'm in the middle of a job here, trying to track down a bunch of owlhoots who have been holding up banks and robbing trains and making general nuisances of themselves for months now, not to mention killing quite a few folks in the process. I ain't got time to hold the hand of some gal who wants to see where her granddaddy once lived."

The young woman's face grew hard with anger. "That's not what this is about, Marshal Long. I assure you, I'm very serious—"

"So am I, Miss . . . what is your name, anyway?"

Her chin jutted toward him defiantly. "It's Kelly. Melinda Kelly."

"Well, Miss Kelly, I'm sorry, but I can't help you, except to tell you that I'd stay out of that desert if I was you. It's no place for a woman."

"That's why I haven't attempted to go out there alone, but no one around here is willing to go with me—"

"I reckon that's because they've all got more sense than to agree to such a thing." Longarm tugged on the brim of his hat. "Now I'll say good evening to you, Miss Kelly. I got to be going."

She started to say something else, then stopped and let out an exasperated sigh instead, as if she were giving up. Longarm sincerely hoped that was the case.

He strode back down the street to the place he had left the marshal—Hogan, the girl said his name was—and saw the lawman standing there, near the public well where Longarm intended to fill his canteens. Instead of the dour expression Hogan had worn earlier, the marshal now had a slight smile on his face.

"I saw you talking to Miss Kelly," he commented as Longarm walked up.

"Yeah. She seems to have a burr under her saddle about this Abaddon place. She from around here?"

Hogan shook his head. "No, she just showed up on the stagecoach one day about a month ago. She asked me to take her into the desert and help her find Abaddon, and when I told her I couldn't do that, she wanted me to recommend somebody she could hire. Problem is, there's not anybody around here willing to go traipsing off into the desert on some wild-goose chase. Even if you knew where the town used to be, you might wander around out there for weeks or even months without ever finding it."

"She ever tell you why she wants to find the place?"

Hogan shook his head. "No. She just says that it's a matter of family business." He paused. "To tell you the truth, Marshal, she's made quite a nuisance of herself. I wish she'd just go back wherever she came from. Maybe she will, now that you've refused to help her, too. You *did* refuse to help her, didn't you?"

"I can't take some girl with me while I'm chasing after outlaws. That's what I told her, too."

"That's what I figured you'd say. I'd do the same thing in your place, Marshal."

Despite the fact that he knew he was right to have turned down Melinda Kelly's request, thoughts of her kept nagging at Longarm's brain as he filled the four canteens and then hung them on his saddle along with the bag of supplies. Then he took the horse's reins and led the animal along the street to the spot where Marshal Hogan pointed out the beginning of the old wagon road.

"Right there," Hogan said as he pointed to a wide, open space between two buildings. In the moonlight,

Longarm saw that the dirt had been graded down so that it rose slightly at each edge of the old road. He was able to follow it with his eyes as it ran out of town, all the way to the edge of the desert about a quarter of a mile away.

Hogan went on, "In the old days, it ran pretty much due west, all the way across the desert, so if you're any good at steering by the stars, you ought to be able to follow it fairly closely even though you won't be able to see it anymore."

"This isn't the spot where Garth and the other two rode out of town," said Longarm.

"No, but all they'd have to do is angle north a little to hit the old road. If they did, you should be able to see their tracks." Hogan shrugged. "If they didn't, you may have to wait until morning to pick up their trail."

"This is worth a try, since Garth talked about the old road."

Hogan held out a hand. "Good luck to you, then, Marshal."

"Much obliged for your help," said Longarm as he shook hands with the local lawman. "And for the good wishes."

"Between the desert and those owlhoots," said Hogan, "I reckon you'll need all the luck you can get."

As it happened, Longarm had plenty of experience at the sort of celestial navigation Marshal Hogan had mentioned, so once he entered the desert and the markings of the road disappeared in a sea of sand, he was able to keep moving in the same direction with a fair degree of confidence.

He hadn't gone more than half a mile into the desert when he spotted the hoofprints angling in from the south.

There wasn't much wind at the moment, so the shifting sand hadn't covered them yet. A tight grin tugged at Longarm's mouth as he saw the tracks turn and head off to the west. Garth knew about the old road, all right, and somehow he'd been able to figure out where it was, maybe by lining it up with the lights of the settlement, which were still visible back to the east.

It hadn't been a bad night's work, reflected Longarm. He had killed three of the outlaws, cutting the membership of the gang in half. And by forcing Garth, Thompson, and Dumont to flee without making the preparations they had intended, he had trapped them. The horses they had stolen might have a canteen or two on them, but it was highly unlikely the outlaws would have enough water to make it all the way across the desert. They might not have any water at all, in which case they would probably have to give up their flight and turn back toward Brimstone the next day. It was possible, thought Longarm, that he could just stop and sit right where he was, waiting for the outlaws to come and surrender before they died of thirst.

Longarm didn't much cotton to the idea of sitting and waiting, though. Never had. So he would push on. But he'd have to keep his eyes open. Colonel Garth was big and dumb-looking, but the way the gang had eluded capture for months so far told Longarm that Garth was actually pretty smart. He might figure that Longarm would come after them, and it was entirely possible that the three of them had stopped somewhere up ahead and were waiting to ambush him at this very moment, thinking that he might have brought enough water with him to get them through to the other side.

There was one other possibility, Longarm realized. Garth and his companions might stumble over what was left of Abaddon and somehow dig out that old well. Maybe the springs were still there. Maybe plenty of water still waited, somewhere under all that sand.

The dry desert air gave up the day's heat quickly. Longarm watched the almost full moon rise higher in the sky, casting its chilly, silvery light over the barren landscape. By midnight, it was pretty cool out there. By morning, it would be downright cold.

It was easier to travel like this, though, than during the middle of the day when the heat was so bad that it seemed to suck all the juices from a man's body and the sun beat down so fiercely it threatened to fry his head like an egg. Longarm pushed on as the moon reached its zenith and began to descend and the stars continued to wheel through the heavens on their inexorable course. The tracks left by the outlaws were still visible, and so were the occasional piles of droppings left by the stolen horses. Longarm checked those droppings from time to time and estimated that Garth and the others were still about an hour ahead of him. They didn't seem to be stopping to set up an ambush. From the looks of it, they wanted to push as deep into the desert as they could before sunup.

So did he. He didn't stop until the moon went down. By then, his horse was played out, and so was he. Longarm let the animal drink a little water that he poured into his hat. He had bought some grain and a nose bag back at the general store in Brimstone, because there wasn't going to be much grass out here for grazing, if any. He planned to wait until morning to feed the horse, though.

In this sand, he couldn't picket his mount, so he tied a rope to the horse's bridle and then to the saddle instead, once he had taken the McClellan off the horse's back. Then he rolled up in his blanket, pillowed his head on the saddle, and settled down to sleep for a couple of hours.

Dawn spreading over the sandy wasteland woke Longarm. He sat up, breathing deeply of the dry, cold air. Then his eyes narrowed and he tipped his head back to look up as a shadow passed by on the ground. A large, black bird had just glided over him.

"Sorry, old son," Longarm called to the bird. "I ain't buzzard bait just yet."

He chuckled as he got to his feet and watched the buzzard continue winging its way westward. He supposed he was lucky that a whole flock of the varmints hadn't decided that he was dead as he lay there sleeping.

Now that it was light, he could see a small patch of scrubby brush about fifty yards away. That brush would provide fuel for a small, almost smokeless fire. Longarm boiled coffee, fried bacon and flapjacks. It was a simple meal but a good one, and along with the sleep he had gotten, it went a long way toward reviving him. He fed and watered the horse, being careful not to give the animal too much, then saddled up and got ready to ride.

The sun was only a hand's width above the horizon when he set out. He would be able to follow the outlaws' trail for several hours before the sun rose too high and got too hot for him to continue. Then he would have to hunt for a place where he could get into the shade during the worst part of the day. The consolation was that Garth, Thompson, and Dumont would have to deal with the heat, too, and in all likelihood, they were in worse shape than he was.

He had been riding for less than an hour when he spotted movement ahead and frowned. The movement he saw wasn't on the ground. It was in the sky, which had begun to take on a hazy, yellowish tint. Black dots wheeled around and around, and as Longarm drew nearer, they turned from dots into birds, the same sort of carrion-feeder as the one that had checked him out earlier. That same buzzard might well be one of the ones circling up there, thought Longarm.

From the looks of it, the buzzards had their beady little eyes on something south of the old wagon road. Probably an animal of some sort, Longarm told himself. Maybe a jackrabbit or a coyote that had strayed too far into the desert and hadn't been able to get back out. Whatever it was, it was none of his business.

Yet he couldn't shake the thought that it might be one of the men he was after lying out there, waiting to die. The outlaws could have gotten separated. One of them might have been thrown from his horse, or his horse could have collapsed, and the other two had abandoned him. Longarm grimaced as he realized that he couldn't just ride on by without stopping to find out.

He turned his horse away from the route of the old road and trotted toward the circling buzzards. After a few minutes, he was able to see something lying on the sandy ground up ahead. Reining in, Longarm took a pair of field glasses from his saddlebags and lifted them to his eyes. He peered through the lenses, twisting the knob to adjust them and bring the distant figure into focus.

He saw right away that the man wasn't Garth or Thompson. He was too small for that. Might be Iron Mike Dumont, thought Longarm, but he didn't really believe that was the case. If he was right, the man was a stranger, probably somebody who'd been foolish enough to try to cross the desert alone and had his horse run away from him. Something like that. The man wasn't moving, either, so he was probably already dead. In a few more minutes, the buzzards would begin to descend on him . . .

Then the man's leg moved. Longarm saw it plainly through the field glasses.

"Well, hell," the big lawman said with a sigh. He had already veered off the trail of his quarry, and he was sure those owlhoots were increasing their lead on him as he hesitated here. Now he had to choose between returning to the old road to continue pursuing the fugitives, or stopping to help some pilgrim who was probably just going to die anyway.

Thinking about it took Longarm all of five seconds. Then he muttered, "Sorry, Billy," and heeled his horse into motion toward the man on the ground.

It didn't take him long to reach the spot where he lay. The man was stretched out on his back, with a battered old black hat covering his face. That shielded his face from the sun. He must have been aware enough of what was going on around him to have heard the hoofbeats of Longarm's horse, because he had started to move around a little by the time Longarm dismounted. Longarm heard a muffled voice ask in cracked tones, "Who . . . who's there . . . ? Somebody . . . ? I need . . . water . . ."

Longarm took one of the canteens off the saddle and went over to hunker on his heels beside the stranger. He positioned himself so that his own body blocked the sun. That allowed him to lift the old hat and get a look at the man's face.

It was burned and blistered by the fierce rays, and lean almost to the point of gauntness. Silvery beard stubble dotted the man's cheeks and jaw. His hair was shot through with gray. Longarm put his age in the forties, maybe the fifties. Maybe even older than that, he decided as he saw how leathery the man's skin was. It looked like a lizard's hide.

The man wore a dirty, gray-striped shirt that had seen better days, as well as canvas trousers and a black vest that were equally old and ragged. A heavy, long-barreled Remington revolver was stuck in an old holster on his hip. Longarm pegged him as the sort of desert rat who spent most of his life far from civilization—and liked it that way.

Longarm got a hand under the man's head and lifted it, bringing the canteen to his lips with his other hand. "Here's some water, old-timer," he said. "Take it easy, though," he added as the man began to suck greedily at the canteen. "Not too much at first."

The man nodded as Longarm lifted the canteen away from his mouth. "I know," he husked through cracked lips covered with dried blood. "I'm . . . much obliged . . . for your help, mister."

"What's your name?"

"They call me . . . Haygood . . . Haygood McCready." His voice held a distinct twang that Longarm recognized. Haygood McCready came from the mountains of Tennessee, or maybe Arkansas.

"Pleased to make your acquaintance, Haygood. I'm Custis Long." Longarm didn't add that he was a deputy U.S. marshal. McCready wouldn't care. To him, Longarm was just the man with the water.

He gave McCready several more sips from the canteen. McCready closed his eyes and sighed. "Thought I was a goner for sure this time," he said. His voice was a little stronger now. "My mule run off, left me afoot. I thought maybe I could walk outta this here desert, but it's mighty big and hot."

"That's the truth," Longarm agreed. "What were you doing out here, anyway?"

The answer surprised him. McCready licked his cracked lips and said, "Chasin' some . . . no-good owl-hoots. You see . . . I'm . . . a deputy sheriff."

Chapter 4

"A lawman?" Longarm said.

"That's right." McCready's eyes narrowed. "You ain't . . . a desperado . . . are you? I don't recollect . . . ever seein' any reward dodgers . . . with your mush on 'em."

Longarm smiled and shook his head. "No, I ain't an outlaw. Fact of the matter is, I pack a badge like you do, old son."

McCready's bushy eyebrows went up. "Is that a fact?"

"Yeah. Deputy U.S. marshal out of Denver."

"You work for . . . Billy Vail?"

"Sure do. You know him?"

McCready shook his head. "Never met him, but I heard tell of him plenty o' times, from when he rode with the Texas Rangers. I was a Ranger, too, for a spell, 'fore I got a mite stove up and took a deputy's job instead. Help me sit up, will you?"

Longarm slid an arm around McCready's shoulders and lifted the man into a sitting position. Then he stepped back, and as he did so, McCready drew that old Remington and pointed it at him.

"Hold on there," said Longarm with a frown. "There's no need to do that."

"The hell there ain't," rasped McCready. "Feller comes along in the middle of a desert and says he's a lawman, and I'm supposed to just believe that? Hell, you could be one of the gang I'm after."

"I can show you my bona fides," Longarm offered. He had moved the folder from the saddle compartment to his pocket, since he wasn't trying to conceal his true identity anymore.

"Why don't you just go ahead and do that? Best move mighty careful-like, though, when you go to reachin' for them papers."

Longarm did as McCready said. Using his left hand, he took out the leather folder and opened it, then held it where McCready could see the badge pinned to one side and the identification papers on the other.

After a moment, McCready nodded. "Looks real enough, I reckon. I can't make out all the words—I didn't have a whole heap o' schoolin', you know—but I know Uncle Sam's seal when I see it."

"So you'll pouch that hogleg?"

"Yeah, sure." McCready slid the revolver back in its holster.

Longarm pulled his from the cross-draw rig.

"What the hell?" said McCready.

"What's good for the goose is good for the gander, or so they say. You got a badge on *you*, Deputy?"

McCready gave an exasperated sigh. "Hang on. I don't wear it pinned on my shirt or vest 'cause the pin got knocked off a while back and I ain't got it fixed yet." He reached into his shirt pocket and pulled out a battered tin star. As he tossed it to Longarm, he said, "Take a gander at that, you like talkin' about ganders so much."

Longarm caught the badge with his left hand and kept the Colt trained on McCready with the other. The badge was a cheap affair, but that wasn't surprising since a lot of sheriff's offices didn't have much money in their budget. The word "Texas" was etched into the center of the badge, with the words "Deputy" and "Sheriff" arching above and below it.

"What county?" asked Longarm.

"Crockett."

"You're a little ways out of your jurisdiction."

"Not really. I'm in pursuit of some no-good owlhoots who robbed the bank in Ozona. Feller name of Garth and his gang."

Longarm frowned as he handed the badge back to McCready. "Hold on a minute. You mean Colonel Garth?"

"That's the low-down varmint I'm talkin' about. He ain't a real colonel, you know. That's his name."

"Yeah, I know," said Longarm. "I'm chasing the same bunch. What I can't figure out is how in blazes you got ahead of me. I had a shoot-out with the gang in Brimstone last night, killed three of them, and then Garth and the other two lit a shuck out here into the desert."

"Well, you see, I knowed they was comin' this way. One o' Garth's men let it slip to a whore back in Ozona that they was plannin' to use the old wagon road to cross the desert west o' Brimstone. So I rode like hell's own flames was a-lickin' at my heels to get ahead of 'em and set up an ambush." McCready snorted. "Didn't figure on that crazy ol' mule o' mine runnin' off, or no federal star packer comin' along and messin' things up for me."

"Messing things up?" repeated Longarm. "Hell, old son, I just saved your life!"

"Well, there is that, I reckon." McCready held up a hand. "Help me up. We got to get movin'."

Longarm holstered his gun, then clasped the old-timer's wrist and pulled him to his feet. "Moving where? On the trail of Garth and his bunch?"

"Maybe later." McCready jabbed a thumb toward the sky. "Right now we got somethin' a heap bigger to worry about."

Longarm looked up. He hadn't really noticed it while he was talking to McCready, but he realized now that the bright sunshine had grown considerably dimmer. That was because the yellow haze in the air had thickened so much that the sun now appeared to be an orange ball in the sky.

"That there's a sandstorm movin' in," McCready went on. "We got to find some place we can ride it out."

"We can head for Brimstone," suggested Longarm.

The old-timer shook his head. "We'd never make it in time. That sumbitch'll be on us in a hour, maybe less."

Longarm knew McCready was right. "How well do you know this desert?"

"Been acrost it a few times. There ain't much out here."

That's what Longarm had figured. In a matter of moments, the situation had gone from bad to worse to potentially fatal. He and Haygood McCready might well have been doomed as soon as that sandstorm began rolling inexorably toward them.

Even if they survived it, Longarm could forget about following Garth and the other two outlaws. Their tracks would be long gone, blown away by the wind.

Longarm tied the canteen back on the saddle, then swung up onto the horse's back. He held a hand down to

McCready. "Come on," he urged. "We know it won't do any good to go east, so we'll keep on heading west."

"I'll slow you down, ridin' double that way," McCready protested.

"That don't make a whole lot of difference now, does it?"

McCready chuckled through his cracked lips. "No, I reckon it don't." He clasped Longarm's hand. "I'm obliged to you for tryin' to help me, Marshal. Leastways I ain't gonna lie there until I die o' thirst and bake in the sun."

Once McCready was mounted behind him, Longarm sent the horse forward. The animal didn't like all the dust floating in the air and moved skittishly. The sun grew dimmer. Longarm tied his bandana around the lower half of his face, and behind him McCready did the same. Longarm reined in and dismounted long enough to tie the nose bag onto the horse to serve the same purpose of filtering out some of the dust and sand and grit, then they pushed on.

After a while, Longarm couldn't even see the sun anymore when he looked up. The sky was a uniform grayish-yellow, and it loomed over them with an oppressive presence.

"If we don't find some place to get outta this soon," McCready called over the steadily rising wind, "we ain't gonna make it. May have to shoot your horse, huddle up against its belly, and pray!"

Longarm nodded, knowing that the old-timer was right. That would be a last resort, though, and he didn't hold out much hope that it would be successful. The sand would just drift over all three of them and cover them up until they might as well have never been there.

The air was so full of sand that they couldn't see more than a few yards in any direction now. Longarm didn't know if they were still headed west or if the horse was just plodding around in circles. He wasn't sure it mattered anymore.

A few minutes later, the horse stumbled. Its front legs went out from under it. As it crumpled forward, Longarm kicked his feet from the stirrups and slipped out of the saddle. McCready toppled off and rolled several feet away.

The horse fell over on its side and refused to get up when Longarm tugged on the reins. McCready struggled to his feet and urged, "Shoot the critter! Maybe he'll block a little of the sand and the wind!"

That wind was howling now. Grains of sand stabbed at the exposed skin of Longarm's face like a million tiny knives. He tugged his hat brim down as far as he could in an attempt to shield his eyes from the onslaught, but it didn't help much.

"If I shoot the horse, we'll be afoot!" he told McCready. "Then we'll never get out of here once the storm blows over!"

"We ain't a-gonna live long enough for it to blow over!" the old-timer shouted back.

Longarm pulled on the reins again. "Come on, damn you!" he urged.

This time, the horse struggled to rise. It took him a couple of minutes, but he managed to get up on his hooves at last.

"He can't carry us any farther!" said Longarm. "I'll lead him." He turned so that the horse was between him and the wind. McCready crowded behind him, taking advantage of what little shelter the horse's body offered.

The three of them trudged along. Since the storm had been blowing in from the west, Longarm thought they were going north now, but he couldn't even be sure of that.

The wind became so fierce that the horse staggered and could barely stay upright. Suddenly, it panicked and jerked hard on the reins, pulling them out of Longarm's grip. He lunged for them, trying to grab them again, but missed. The horse turned and ran, putting its rump to the wind. In only a couple of seconds, Longarm couldn't even see the animal anymore and knew there was no point in trying to chase it.

"Son of a . . ." he muttered.

"We're dead men now," said McCready. "Might as well set ourselves down right here and let the sand have us."

"The hell with that!" said Longarm. "I'm gonna keep moving as long as I can!"

"Why?"

"Why not?"

McCready grinned as he used one hand to hold his battered old hat on his head. "Well, I reckon when you put it that way, there ain't no good reason why not. Hadn't we ought to tie ourselves together somehow, to keep from gettin' separated?"

That was a good idea. Longarm used his belt to tie his left wrist to McCready's right wrist. The deputy sheriff didn't like having his gun arm hindered like that, but the odds of them getting in a gunfight in the middle of a terrible sandstorm like this were pretty small. McCready had to admit that.

Once the two men were linked, they trudged forward again. Longarm had no idea which direction they were moving now. North, south, east, and west no longer had any meaning out here. There was only the churning sand that filled the air, scoured the skin, clogged the eyes and nose and mouth, choked the lungs.

Longarm had no idea how long they stumbled around the desert. He wasn't thinking clearly anymore. His only thought was to keep moving. If anyone had asked him why that was so important, he wouldn't have been able to tell them. He was operating on pure instinct now, not on any sort of rational thought. He was only barely aware that he and McCready were slogging up a fairly steep slope, as if they were climbing a giant sand dune.

Suddenly, his right foot hit something hard. That was so unexpected, Longarm stumbled and almost fell. He put his hand out to catch himself, felt his palm scrape against something rough.

"What is it?" yelled McCready, who must have felt Longarm break stride. "What's wrong, Marshal?"

For an instant when Longarm bumped into the unknown object, the thought that it was a rock had flashed through his mind. Touching it with his hand told him it was something else. The texture wasn't that of stone. He ran both hands over it now, and jerked one back as pain bit into a finger.

He had picked up a splinter, Longarm realized. He had stumbled into something made out of wood.

"There's something here!" he shouted to McCready. "I think maybe it's a piece of an old wagon!"

"Is it big enough for us to get behind it?"

"I don't know!" Longarm brushed more sand away from the planks, which lay buried at an angle. "Maybe!"

He dropped to his knees so that he could work better, and so did McCready. As they cleared a bigger space, Longarm spotted a metal bar jutting up several feet in the air. Since he thought the boards were part of a wagon bed, that had to be part of the frame. He pointed out the bar to McCready and said, "Let's tie ourselves to that and see if we can wait out the storm! I think we must be at the top of a dune, because the sand's not piling up too much around us!"

"Danged if I don't think you're right! Use that belt o' yours!"

Longarm followed the old-timer's advice. They sat on each side of the iron bar and he looped his belt around it and one arm on each of them. Then they grabbed the bar and hung on for dear life, as if the wind that was howling and screeching like a living thing might pick them up and carry them away if they didn't. Longarm wasn't completely sure that it wouldn't, even if they did hang on.

The wind-driven sand scoured them. They had their bandanas completely covering their faces now. Longarm drew his knees up, hunched forward, and tried to curl himself into as small a ball as he could manage. That would give the sand less of a target, he reasoned.

After a while, he couldn't see McCready anymore, even though he could have reached out and touched the old-timer. If McCready said anything, Longarm didn't hear it. He didn't hear anything except the wind. Nothing existed in the world except the wind and the sand and the desperate struggle to draw a little air through the bandana without swallowing a mouthful of grit to go with it.

Incredibly, even under these extreme circumstances, exhaustion claimed Longarm after a while. He didn't really sleep, wasn't exactly unconscious, but he wasn't aware of anything, either. He was in a shadowy, twilight world, hovering somewhere between life and death.

And while Longarm was lost in that wasteland of unawareness, the storm moved on.

A groan came from deep within him as he emerged from the stupor that had gripped him. The first thing he realized was that the howling wind had stopped. Only a light breeze blew now, caressing his cheek where the bandana had pulled back a little.

He saw light against his eyelids, too, and tried to force them open. They didn't want to cooperate. Sand had glued them shut. He had to lift a shaking hand and wipe some of it away, which just irritated his eyes that much more. Tears flowed somehow and washed away more of the sand. His eyelids fluttered open.

Weak, pale sunlight washed over the boards on which he lay. He moved his head enough to look up, and so much sand still floated in the air that he could still look directly at the orange ball of the sun. It was low to the horizon, so he knew that must be west. The sun had to be setting instead of coming up; he hadn't been lying here long enough for an entire night to have gone by. At least, he didn't think so.

He wondered if Haygood McCready was still alive, or if the deputy sheriff had been smothered to death in the sandstorm. Longarm still had an elbow looped around the iron bar that stuck up from the planks. He started trying to pull himself up by it, but he was so weak he could barely manage to move.

Suddenly, he heard a squeaking sound somewhere above his head. Not having any idea what could be causing that, he tipped his head back and peered upward with bleary, red-rimmed eyes. A jolt of surprise went through him when he saw an arrow cut out of tin and attached to the end of the bar. Clutching that arrow with tin claws was the silhouette of a rooster.

The bar wasn't part of a wagon, Longarm realized. It

wasn't even a bar. It was a pole. And on top of that pole was a damn weather vane. But that made no sense at all, he thought, because weather vanes were usually on top of roofs . . .

And so was he. Longarm looked around in shock and saw that the storm had cleared away the rest of the sand. He and McCready, who lay senseless or maybe dead on the other side of the pole, weren't on top of a dune after all. They were lying at the peak of a roof, with a building underneath them. That wasn't all.

Longarm turned his head, gazing in amazement at the other buildings, at least half a dozen of them, in some disrepair but remarkably intact. Those buildings hadn't been there before the storm, he told himself—or at least, they hadn't been visible.

They had been buried, until the howling winds had come along to uncover them.

Longarm and McCready had found Abaddon.

Chapter 5

As soon as he recovered a little from the shock of his discovery, Longarm reached over and shook McCready's shoulder. "McCready!" he called. "Wake up, McCready!"

The old-timer stirred slightly. Breath rasped in his throat. Longarm shoved him again and said, "Haygood!"

"Dadgummit, don't . . . don't be a-hollerin' at me like that, Pa. I'll get up and do the plowin' directly, I swear I will . . ."

"Deputy McCready!"

That didn't get through to him, either. Longarm sighed in exasperation. He untied the belt that held him to both McCready and the weather vane and used the pole to help himself stand up. Once he was on his feet and holding on to the pole to steady himself, he was able to take a good look around.

They were only a few feet from the end of the building, which stretched out a good fifty or sixty feet in the other direction. This was the biggest structure in town and had what appeared to be a slightly newer wing built on one side, so Longarm figured it had probably been

O'Sullivan's trading post, saloon, and whorehouse.

From the location of the other buildings, he judged that Abaddon had had only one street, and that street had been only a block long. Two other buildings sat on this side of it, with four structures of various sizes facing them from the other side.

All the buildings were made out of thick planks that must have been freighted out here at considerable cost. They were gray and pitted from exposure to the elements, but one thing about being in the middle of a desert, wood didn't rot very quickly and there weren't all that many bugs to gnaw on it. While Abaddon had been covered up, the sand had acted to preserve the buildings.

"Well, I'll be a lop-eared mule!" exclaimed McCready. "Danged if I won't!"

Longarm looked over his shoulder and saw that the deputy sheriff finally had woken up enough to realize where they were. McCready was staring around with eyes that appeared to be about to pop out of their sockets.

"How in the name o' all that's holy did we get up here?" he went on. "Did the wind pick us up and drop us right on top o' this here buildin'?"

Longarm shook his head. "This is where we were all along. That dune we were climbing just before we found what we thought was a piece of wagon was really covering this building."

"But . . . but that ain't rightly possible!"

Longarm waved a hand at their surroundings. "What other explanation have you got? This is that old ghost town Abaddon. It was covered up by sand, and the storm came along and uncovered it."

"Abaddon . . ." McCready repeated softly. "I recollect hearin' about the place. This is it? You're sure?"

"I don't think there are any other towns in the middle of this desert," said Longarm.

"No . . . No, I reckon you're right about that." McCready shook his head. "I never woulda dreamed it, though."

"Me, neither," agreed Longarm.

He studied the terrain around the old abandoned settlement. It was mostly flat to the east and south, although some small dunes gave the tan-and-brown landscape a rolling aspect. To the north and west were a pair of low, rocky ridges at right angles to each other. Other than that, the desert was open, barren, and ugly.

McCready got up and came over to join him. The old-timer was a little unsteady, and as he swayed, Longarm reached out to grasp his arm and brace him.

"I never thought we'd live through that sandstorm."

"I had a few doubts my own self," said Longarm.

"What do we do now? Looks like we got about a hour o' daylight left. We better figure out a way down offa here." McCready paused, then went on. "Don't reckon it really matters, though. We can die o' thirst a-sittin' up here just as easy as we can anywheres else."

"We ain't gonna die of thirst."

McCready squinted over at Longarm. "Your hoss ran away, remember? And he had all the canteens on him. We're afoot, in the middle of this here desert, with no water. Sounds like a pure-dee death sentence to me."

"There's water here," said Longarm. "We just have to find it."

"How do you figure that?"

Longarm hunkered down on his heels and studied what was left of the town of Abaddon. "This place was started by a man named O'Sullivan," he explained. "He knew there were some springs out here, so he came to find them. When he did, he put in a well and a trading post, and then he ran the wagon road right beside it. The well never ran dry; it just kept getting clogged up with sand, so that O'Sullivan had to dig it out again. It should still be here somewhere."

"Just because it didn't run dry whilst this feller O'Sullivan was tryin' to make a go of the settlement, that don't mean it hasn't since then," argued McCready. "Even if we could find that ol' well, it's been a-sittin' there plumb full o' sand for years and years now."

Longarm grinned wearily. "Then we'll have a lot of digging to do to find out, won't we?"

"No offense, Marshal, but that just sounds addlepated to me. How'd we even know where to start lookin'?"

Longarm stood up and brushed his hands together, getting some of the sand off them. "O'Sullivan would have built the trading post as close to the well as he could, to make it easy to carry water. Let's see if we can get down off this building and have a look around."

Feeling stronger and steadier on his feet now, he went to the edge of the roof and looked over it, and saw that the building had a front porch that ran the full length of it. Thick wooden beams held up the part of the roof that extended out over the porch. Longarm was able to lie down with his legs dangling off the edge and carefully lower himself until he could wrap his legs around one of the beams. From there he shinnied down it to the ground.

McCready watched the operation with a dubious look on his leathery face. "I ain't sure I can do that," he said.

"Just hang from the edge and drop," Longarm suggested. "It's not that far."

McCready shook his head. "These old bones o' mine might not be able to take all that joltin' and jouncin' around."

"Well, hold on, then," said Longarm. "I'll go inside and take a look around. Maybe I can find an old ladder or something."

The door lay on the porch, the hinges that had held it on having rusted away. Longarm stepped inside the shadowy interior of the trading post. Out of habit, his hand was ready to reach for his gun. He never entered a strange place without being careful . . . although considering that this one had been completely covered up with sand a few hours ago, he didn't think it was very likely that anybody would be waiting in there to bushwhack him.

The trading post was empty, all right, except for piles of sand everywhere. Even where the sand hadn't drifted, it was so thick on the floor that walking through it was like slogging through the desert itself.

He found an empty barrel in one of the back rooms and rolled it out to the porch. Setting it up next to one of the porch supports, he told McCready, "You'll be able to let yourself down and stand on the barrel, and then you can climb down from there with that beam to hold on to."

"I reckon I could do that," McCready agreed.

"I'll be right here to give you a hand if you need it."

Carefully, McCready descended from the porch roof. When his worn old boots touched the porch planks, he heaved a sigh and said, "Feels mighty good to be on solid ground again."

"I'm not sure how solid this sand is, considering the way it shifts around when the wind blows," said Longarm, "but I know what you mean."

McCready ran his tongue over his cracked lips. "I was

plumb cotton-mouthed already, and now I feel like if I don't get a drink soon, my insides is a-gonna shrivel up and crumble to dust."

Longarm knew how the old-timer felt. He was parched, too, and even though he'd been trying to ignore that while they got down off the roof, he knew the situation was desperate.

"Let's see if we can find that well," he said.

They started by circling the building. At the eastern end, Longarm saw a large hump in the sand. He started digging at it with his bare hands.

"You think that's it?" McCready asked.

"There's a door in the end of the building right here," Longarm pointed out. "That would be handy for carrying in water if this is the well. It didn't get completely uncovered in this storm because the building itself blocked some of the wind."

"Ain't very tall."

"Maybe the wall around it eroded over the years."

Longarm continued digging, and after a moment, McCready pitched in to help. After about ten minutes, Longarm uncovered part of a rock. It looked like red sandstone, quarried maybe on one of those nearby ridges.

Longarm didn't think about how thirsty he was. He just kept digging. As he and McCready uncovered more rocks, a circular wall began to take shape.

"This is it!" McCready said. "Has to be!"

"Yeah," Longarm agreed. "It's full of sand, too, just like we thought it would be."

"We're gonna need shovels." McCready didn't sound so pessimistic now. He had a shred of hope to cling to, and that was all most people needed.

"I can bust up one of those old counters inside the trad-

ing post. Some pieces of board will be better than nothing
for digging."

Longarm hurried inside to do that. He kicked one of
the display counters apart and came back out with two
broken pieces of board small enough for him and
McCready to handle. The well was wide enough across
for both of them to stand in it once they stepped over the
wall. The two men went to their knees and started scooping up sand on the boards and flinging it out of the well as
fast as they could.

Longarm had no idea how far down the springs were,
if indeed they still existed at all. The sand was packed
fairly tightly in the well, so the digging wasn't as easy as
he had hoped it would be. He and McCready kept it up
stubbornly, though, even as the light began to fade from
the sky.

"I'll   all night if I have to," McCready said. "I got to
have water."

"Save your breath for digging," Longarm advised.

The deeper they got, the harder it was to throw the
sand out of the hole they were creating. Some of it went
out, but some fell back in, so they just had to scoop it up
again. After a while, Longarm said, "This ain't gonna
work. We need some way to haul the sand up out of here."

"Take your shirt off," McCready suggested. "We'll
make a sack out of it."

Longarm nodded. That was a good idea. He stripped
the shirt off, tied the sleeves closed at the ends, and tied
the bottom of it as well. Once it was buttoned up, they
were able to scoop sand in through the neck and fill the
shirt. A little trickled back out, but not much.

When Longarm stood up, he could reach high enough
to dump the sand in the shirt outside the well. After a

while, though, as the hole continued to deepen, his arms wouldn't stretch that far anymore.

"Climb out," he told McCready. "I'll fill the shirt and toss it up to you. You can empty it and throw it back down to me."

"All right."

Longarm made a stirrup out of his hands and boosted McCready out of the well. The old-timer looked back down over the wall with a frown on his face.

"If it keeps gettin' deeper and deeper, how're you gonna get back out once you hit water?"

"We'll figure that out when the time comes. Right now let's just find the water."

Longarm thought the sandstone blocks that formed the well's shaft were irregular enough so that he could climb out. If not, maybe McCready could tear up the shirt and make a rope out of it. Like he had told the deputy sheriff, they would figure out something.

Stars had winked into existence as the sky deepened from blue to purple to black above the well. Longarm was a good twenty feet down, scooping sand into the shirt with his hands, when he suddenly felt something that hadn't been there before.

Moisture.

His breath hissed between his teeth as he dug his fingers deeper into the dirt. It wasn't sand now, so much as it was mud, he realized as his heart leaped. His hands dug frenziedly.

"Mud!" he shouted up to McCready. "I've got mud!"

"Saints be praised!" the old-timer's reedy voice exclaimed. "You want me to come down there?"

"No! Stay where you are."

"You ain't a-gonna try to hog all that water for yourself, now are ye, Marshal?"

"Take it easy," said Longarm. "Let me see what we've got here."

He dug a match out of his pocket and snapped the lucifer to life with an iron-hard thumbnail. As the match flared, the yellow glow it cast showed him the dark spot on the sand where he knelt. With his free hand, he scooped out more of the mud, making a small hole only a few inches across. As he watched, muddy water began to seep into that hole, forming a tiny pool.

"The springs are still here," he said. "All I have to do is dig down a little farther."

And figure out a way to get the water to the top of the well, he thought.

"You have any matches?" he called up to McCready.

"Nary a one."

"Hold on." Longarm always carried a little watertight container in which were several lucifers. He took it out of his pocket and said, "I'll toss some up to you. See if you can find a lantern, or make a torch, or something like that, and start searching the buildings. We need a bucket and some rope."

"All right. I'm ready."

Longarm tossed the matches to the top of the well. It took a couple of tries before McCready caught the little container.

"I'll be back," the old-timer promised.

"I'll keep digging."

Longarm piled the excess sand around the edges of the shaft now, since he was concentrating on making the smaller hole deeper. As he worked, he scooped up some of the muddy water and sucked it into his mouth. The dirt in it didn't taste good, but the moisture was more than welcome. In fact, it was a blessed relief to his parched lips, mouth, and throat. He felt a little bad about drinking when McCready hadn't had a chance to yet, but that didn't stop him.

After a while he had a hole about a foot wide and a couple of feet deep. He sat back, leaning against the sandstone wall of the shaft, and let the water from the springs trickle into the hole. From time to time he reached down and felt the growing puddle in the bottom of the hole. If the springs were still strong enough to fill the hole, the sand would settle to the bottom and he and McCready would be left with relatively clear water.

He must have dozed off, because he came awake with a start as McCready called down to him, "I found an old bucket! It leaks a mite, but it was the best I could find."

"Can you lower it down to me?"

"Yeah. Sorry, Marshal, but I had to tear up your shirt to make a rope."

Longarm chuckled. He didn't tell McCready that he had been thinking about the very same thing earlier.

"That's fine. Lower it down here, and I'll send it back up with some water in it for you."

"Here it comes."

Longarm saw McCready's dark shape against the starlight as the old-timer leaned over the well. He was able to make out the bucket as it descended on the makeshift rope, too, and stood up to take hold of it as it reached him.

"Got it! Wait a minute, and I'll tell you when to pull it up again."

The bucket was small enough so that he could turn it sideways, put it down in the hole, and let some of the water that had gathered run into it. When he had enough in the bucket that it sloshed a little as he took it out of the hole, he called, "All right, take it up! Just be careful."

"I reckon you can count on that," said McCready.

Longarm felt a few drops spatter down on his bare torso as the bucket rose through the shaft. Then McCready had it at the top, and Longarm heard the deputy sheriff drinking greedily, sucking down the muddy water. After a moment, McCready let out a long sigh and said, "Lord have mercy, I reckon that was the pure-dee tastiest water I ever drunk in all my borned days, mud and all."

"Yeah, I felt the same way." Longarm hunkered down on his heels by the hole and reached into it. The water on the bottom was several inches deep now and still trickling in. "I think I'll dig a little deeper and see if I can get it flowing faster."

"You be careful down there! You don't want to block up them springs again!"

"Don't worry," Longarm said as he leaned over, filled both hands with mud from the bottom of the hole, and pulled them out. He cast the mud aside and went back for more.

After digging for a few minutes, he thought the water was running faster into the hole. Something else struck him as different, too. He plunged his hands into the water again and felt a definite warmth against his fingers as he dug them into the mud. In fact, the water flowing into the hole was starting to get downright hot.

"Oh, hell," Longarm whispered.

If this was a hot spring, that meant it would have some pressure built up behind it. He was no expert on geology, but he knew that from time to time there was some volcanic activity in this region. That meant the heat from the living core of the earth could reach close to the surface and cause the water to be so hot that it had to find some place to go. Normally, that pressure bled off through natu-

ral springs and artesian wells, but this particular spring
had been blocked up for a long time . . .

"Haygood!" Longarm shouted. "Drop me that rope!"

"What? You want the bucket again?"

"The rope! I need the rope! I gotta get out of here!"

"What the Sam Hill are you talkin' about, Marshal?"

"This well . . . it's about to turn into a damn geyser!"

Under his feet, Longarm felt a tiny vibration. At the
same time, a faint rumble from deep in the earth came to
his ears. Somewhere below him, there might well be tons
of water and steam seeking a path out of their long con-
finement. Unwittingly, he had given it all a way to escape.

And now he was right in its deadly path.

Chapter 6

"The rope!" Longarm shouted again. He still thought he could climb up the side of the well if he had to, but that would take too long. He didn't have much time.

"Hang on!" called McCready. "Here it comes!"

Longarm felt the tied-together strips of his shirt brush against his face as the makeshift rope fell into the shaft. He grabbed it and tugged on it, hoping it was strong enough to hold his weight. It was fine for raising and lowering a little bucket, but supporting a big man was something entirely different.

The ground was still shaking under his feet, harder now, and the rumbling noise was getting louder. "Are you set up there?" he called to McCready.

"Sittin' down and braced as best I can with my feet against the well," replied the deputy sheriff. "Best get on outta there, Marshal, 'fore that thing blows!"

Longarm couldn't have agreed more. Trusting to the makeshift rope because he didn't have any other choice, he tightened his grip on it, raised a foot and planted it against the sandstone wall, and started walking up the close-fitted blocks of stone. He leaned far back, taking most of his weight on his arms and shoulders, and grunted from the strain of it as he climbed.

Suddenly, he felt a hot wind blowing up from below him, as if a door into Hell had just swung open. The breach he had started must have widened. Hauling hard, pushing upward with his feet as much as he could, he went hand-over-hand up the rope. He was halfway to the top, leaving only about ten feet to cover. He might not have time for that ten feet, though, because he felt a hot spray of water strike his back. The heat was bearable right now, but soon it would be scalding, then boiling, and if he was caught in the geyser, it might well cook the meat right off his bones . . .

The rope slipped a little, and he fell back a couple of inches. "Hang on!" he bellowed to McCready.

"Sorry! I got it!"

Longarm kept climbing. He wasn't going to give up as long as there was breath in his body. Abruptly, he realized that he had reached the top of the well. He got his right foot on top of the wall and shoved hard with it, lifting himself until his body was above the level of the opening.

With a sudden roar, water exploded up through the shaft. But at the same time, Longarm let out a roar of his own and dived clear of the well. He hit the ground hard and rolled over, looking back to see the column of water rising from the well and spreading out in a spray that fell like hot, stinging rain. Longarm and McCready both scrambled away from it.

"Lordy!" said McCready. "I never seen nothin' like that in all my borned days!"

"I have, up in the Yellowstone country," said Longarm. "What they used to call Colter's Hell. I was never this close to any of those geysers, though."

The force of this one was already dying down, now that the pressure was off. The water cooled as it hit the night air, and it turned the sandy ground around the well to mud. Longarm knew that once the water stopped erupting, the sand would soak up the moisture that had fallen on it, and by morning the ground would once again be as dry as if this had never happened.

But with luck, the well itself would be full, and although the water might be a little warmer than usual because it was fed by hot springs, it wouldn't be scalding anymore. He and McCready could roll that barrel over there and use the bucket to fill it, and they would have a good supply of drinking water for a while, anyway.

But they were still trapped in the middle of the burning desert, with no real way out.

They might well have traded the relatively quick death of thirst for the longer ordeal of starvation.

There was no point in thinking about that now, though. Things could change, Longarm told himself. He and McCready might find a way out of this yet.

McCready started to laugh. "You like to got your ass scalded off," he said. "You come jumpin' up outta that well like a damn jack-in-the-box."

"That's kind of the way I felt," Longarm said with a chuckle of his own. He held out a hand and let the spray from the well come down on it. "Feel that? The water's cooling off already. That must be an artesian spring down there, with some natural pressure that got worse the more it heated up. It's not normally all that hot, though. That's why O'Sullivan was able to use it. He'd have made an oasis out of this place if he'd only been able to keep the sand from plugging up the well."

"Why do you reckon he never put a buildin' over it?"

mused McCready. "That would've kept the sand out, wouldn't it?"

Longarm nodded. "You'd think so. Maybe he just never thought of it. A man can be mighty smart but still have some blind spots he don't even know about."

"Yeah, I reckon. If the feller's dead, I don't guess we'll ever know."

Longarm moved closer to the well so that the spray would wash over him. Although the water was still warm, it felt good as it trickled over his face and torso and washed away some of the dust that had coated him like a second skin. Next to him, McCready took off his hat and held it so that it caught water in it. When the hat was almost full, he upended it over his head and let the water cascade down over him. McCready let out a howl of pleasure.

After a few more minutes, the geyser stopped. Longarm went over to the well and peered down into it. The shaft was full of water halfway to the top. The level might still be climbing slowly, too; the moonlight wasn't bright enough for him to be sure.

"We ain't a-gonna die of thirst, looks like," said McCready, unwittingly echoing the thought that had gone through Longarm's head earlier. "We're still in a bad fix, though."

"I know. But there's nothing we can do about it tonight, so I don't intend to worry about it right now."

"That's just about the most smartest thing I ever heard. I figure on drinkin' my fill and then gettin' some sleep. We'll worry about what to do next come mornin'."

McCready had tossed aside the bucket when he threw the rope down to Longarm. Now they found it again and used it to haul up enough water to quench their thirst.

Longarm's belly growled from lack of food, but he told it to hush up.

They went inside the old trading post. McCready brushed as much of the sand off the bar in the saloon as he could, then said, "This here is gonna be my bed. Won't be the first time in my life I've slept on a bar, I can tell you that for dang sure. 'Course, I was a mite passed out them other times."

"I'll crawl up on one of those counters in the store," said Longarm. "As long as another storm doesn't come along and bury these buildings again, I reckon we'll be all right."

"Now, doggone it, why'd you have to go and say somethin' like that? Now I'm gonna worry."

Longarm laughed and found one of the counters that looked sturdy enough to support his weight. He lifted himself onto it and stretched out.

"Haygood, you think we ought to take turns standing watch?" he called into the other room as the thought occurred to him.

A resounding snore was the only answer he got from McCready. Longarm laughed softly and sat up. As tired as he was, he knew better than to go to sleep. Garth, Thompson, and Dumont had been out there somewhere on the desert when the giant sandstorm hit. While it was unlikely that they had survived, it wasn't any more unlikely than the fact that Longarm and McCready were still alive. The last thing they needed was to have those outlaws stumble over them without any warning. Garth and the others wouldn't hesitate to kill a couple of lawmen.

So he sat there in the dark and listened to the soft whisper of the wind as it blew lightly outside. Enough of a breeze came through the open front door of the trading post to stir the sand that had collected on the floor. Longarm heard the faint rustling noise that made, too.

After a while it was like the night was singing to him, and considering how close he had come to dying, it was a mighty pretty song.

When Longarm couldn't stay awake anymore, he went into the next room and woke Haygood McCready. He was careful as he did so; some men just naturally reached for a gun if they were roused from a sound sleep. Longarm was ready to grab McCready's wrist if the deputy sheriff tried to slap leather.

McCready woke up fairly peacefully, though. He sat up on the bar, yawned, and said, "It ain't mornin' yet."

"I thought it would be a good idea if one of us stood watch. I've been sitting up in the other room."

"Stand watch? What for? There ain't nobody else out here."

"We can't be sure of that," Longarm pointed out. "We survived that sandstorm. Garth and those other two outlaws might have, too."

McCready scratched at his jaw and then slowly nodded. "Yeah, I reckon you're right. I'm obliged to you for takin' the first turn, Marshal. I was plumb wore to a frazzle."

"I'm getting that way myself."

"You go on and get some sleep," McCready told him. The old-timer slid down from the bar. "I'll keep my eyes open. Might even walk around town a little, just to get the lay o' the land and see if I can find anything we might get some use out of."

"All right, just be careful. And holler if you need me."

"Sure thing." McCready clumped out of the trading post, the spurs on his boots jingling.

Longarm stretched out on the counter, pillowed his head on his arms, and fell almost instantly into a deep, dreamless sleep. Nothing disturbed him, and although he was stiff from lying on the hard counter when he awoke, he also felt refreshed and a little stronger. Still hungry, though.

The sun was shining, but it was still early enough so that some of the night chill lingered in the air, especially for a man with no shirt on. Longarm's shirt had been destroyed to make that rope, and since it had saved his life when he was scrambling out of the well, he thought that was a good enough trade. He'd had a spare shirt in his saddlebags, but it was anybody's guess where his saddle, and the horse it was attached to, were now. Buried under a mound of sand, more than likely.

Longarm checked the other rooms for McCready but didn't see any sign of the deputy sheriff. He stepped outside and looked around. "McCready!" he called. "You out here?"

There was no answer. The silence brought a frown to Longarm's face. He didn't think it was likely that anything had happened to McCready, but he couldn't rule it out. It could be that something as simple as an accident had befallen the deputy sheriff.

Longarm searched the other two buildings on the same side of the street as the trading post without finding McCready. He started across the street toward the other buildings but was only halfway there when the old-timer called from behind him, "You lookin' for me, Marshal?"

Longarm stopped short in surprise and turned around. He looked up and saw McCready standing on the roof, holding on to the pole with the weather vane attached to it.

"Didn't you hear me calling your name?" he asked.

McCready shook his head and pointed to his right ear. "Sometimes these ol' ears o' mine play tricks on me. I heard somethin', but I thought it was just the wind."

Longarm came closer to the building. "What the hell are you doing up there, anyway?"

McCready grinned and held up something that flashed in the morning sunlight. "I found a piece of broken mirror in one o' them other buildin's. Thought I'd climb up here and start signalin' with it. I been flashin' the thing in all directions. If anybody's out there, they'll know there's somebody here at this old settlement."

That was a good idea in a way, thought Longarm. Maybe not so good in another way, since the only people they knew for sure had been in the desert when the storm hit were the three outlaws.

On the other hand, he and McCready couldn't hope to make it back to civilization without horses, and it was possible that Garth's bunch still had their mounts. If they could lure the outlaws to Abaddon, they might be able to take those horses away from them.

That would probably mean killing Garth, Thompson, and Dumont. Remembering how many people they had gunned down in the course of their robberies, Longarm was just fine with that.

He grinned up at McCready and said, "I'm surprised you were able to climb up there, what with those old bones of yours and all."

McCready gibed back. "You just keep a civil tongue in your head, youngster. A feller can do a lot of things when they're liable to save his ornery old hide."

Longarm waved. "Keep signaling. I'm going to look around some more."

It was hard to tell what sort of businesses the other

buildings in Abaddon had housed. A couple of them still sported signs, but all the paint had been scoured off by the sand and wind. Longarm knew that one place had been a blacksmith shop because the forge was still there. The others had been stores of some kind, but that was all he knew.

He was in the building farthest from the trading post when he faintly heard McCready calling, "Marshal! Marshal Long!"

Longarm hurried outside and cupped his hand around his mouth. "What is it?"

McCready pointed toward the east. "Somebody comin'!"

Longarm's heart leaped in his chest. It was unlikely that the three outlaws would be approaching from that direction. This had to be someone else, and maybe they had horses and food and a way out of this desert death trap. Longarm trotted up the street toward the trading post.

When he got there, he climbed up one of the porch posts and pulled himself onto the roof. Making his way carefully to the top, he joined McCready, who was shading his eyes from the glare of the sun with a leathery hand. The fiery orb was still fairly low and made it difficult to see.

"Out yonder," said the deputy sheriff. "Looks like just one feller, and I can't tell if he's afoot or on horseback. He's still too far away."

Longarm shaded his own eyes and squinted in the direction McCready indicated. His spirits sank a little as he picked out the black dot moving against the sand.

"One man, all right," he said, "and what I can see looks too small to be a man on a horse."

"Yeah, I was thinkin' the same thing," said McCready. "One more pilgrim in the same fix we're in ain't gonna help us."

Longarm walked to the other end of the building to check the well, which had been at least three-fourths full of water this morning. At least there would be plenty to drink if the newcomer was thirsty, as he was bound to be in the middle of a desert.

"Think it's one o' them owlhoots?" asked McCready.

"It's possible. They were ahead of me, but I reckon we could have passed them during the storm."

Longarm wished he still had his field glasses. Something struck him as odd about the lone figure trudging toward the settlement, but he couldn't figure out what it was.

"Why don't you signal again?" he suggested. "Just so he'll know for sure that somebody's here and that he's going in the right direction."

"Good idea." McCready lifted the piece of broken mirror and bounced the sun's rays off it, sending the flashes shooting across the desert. Longarm thought the stranger might return the signals, but that didn't happen. The hombre might not have anything shiny enough to use.

Longarm and McCready could see a long way from the top of the trading post. Longarm estimated that the stranger was still at least a quarter of a mile from the settlement when he began weaving back and forth.

McCready noticed that, too. "That don't look too good," he said. "Feller acts like he's got his brain all bollixed up. Either that, or he's just too tired to go on."

"Maybe both," said Longarm. He added, "Son of a bitch!" when the distant figure suddenly slumped to the ground and didn't move again.

"Dead, you reckon?"

"Or passed out. I'd better go find out which."

"I'll come with you."

Longarm shook his head. "You stay up here and keep signaling to all points of the compass. It looks like one person saw those flashes. Somebody else could, too."

"All right, but if you need any help, let off a shot with that hogleg o' yours, and I'll come a-runnin'. Well, maybe not *runnin'* . . ."

Longarm climbed down from the roof. From the ground, he couldn't see the man who had collapsed out on the desert, but he had the line in his head that he needed to follow, so he started trotting in that direction. The buildings of Abaddon fell behind him. In a few minutes, he was sweating from his exertions because the air was already starting to get warm. He wished he had paused to get a good long drink earlier. There would be time for that later, he told himself.

The man he was looking for came into view, a dark shape sprawled on the sand ahead of him and a little to the right. Longarm angled toward the motionless form. As he got closer, a frown creased his forehead. He thought he knew what had seemed odd to him earlier.

The hombre just wasn't shaped right.

The figure was lying on its back, and there were some extra curves on the chest that wouldn't have been there if it belonged to a man. That was definitely a woman's bosom.

But what was a woman doing out here, alone and on foot, in the middle of this godforsaken desert? Who was she, and more importantly, was she still alive?

Longarm got the answers to those last two questions as he reached her and dropped to his knees beside her. She appeared to be unconscious, but her breasts were rising and falling in a steady rhythm under the man's shirt she wore.

And Longarm knew who she was because he had met her back in Brimstone. He was looking down into the lovely face of Melinda Kelly.

Chapter 7

Longarm bent over her and slapped her face lightly to try to bring her around. "Miss Kelly," he said. "Miss Kelly, wake up."

She stirred slightly, but her eyes didn't open and she didn't make a sound.

Longarm looked her over from head to foot to make sure she wasn't injured or bleeding. In addition to the man's shirt—which gapped open slightly between a couple of buttons and revealed an intriguingly rounded bit of female flesh—Melinda wore denim trousers and boots. A brown hat lay nearby on the ground where it had landed when she fell. Longarm wondered if she had finally found someone to bring her out here into the desert, or if she had set off in search of Abaddon on her own.

It didn't matter at the moment. He needed to get her back to the settlement, into the shade where there was water. She probably needed those two things as much as anything right now. On one knee beside her, he leaned forward and slid his arms under her shoulders and her knees, then picked her up and lurched to his feet.

She was slender enough so that normally he wouldn't have had any trouble carrying her. After the wringer he had been through in the past twelve hours, though, and with the hunger that gripped him, he was still skating on the thin edge of exhaustion. He stumbled a little as he turned and started toward Abaddon with Melinda cradled in his arms.

He saw Haygood McCready climbing down from the roof of the trading post. By the time he reached the end of the street, McCready was there waiting for him.

"What in the name of Saint Pete you got there, Marshal?" asked the deputy sheriff.

Longarm summoned up a smile as he continued along the street and McCready fell in step beside him. "Been so long since you've seen a woman that you don't recognize one, Haygood?"

"Oh, I recognize she's a woman, all right, but I sure as shootin' didn't expect to see one out here in the midst o' this here desert."

"Neither did I," said Longarm. "What's even stranger, I know this gal. Her name's Melinda Kelly."

"Melinda Kelly," McCready repeated. "That's a right pretty name . . . and a right pretty gal. Who is she?"

"Her grandfather was William O'Sullivan, the man who put in the well and built the trading post. The founder of Abaddon, I guess you'd say. She introduced herself to me back in Brimstone, because she'd heard that I was coming out here after those owlhoots, and she wanted me bring her with me."

"What? Why, if that ain't the most dad-blasted loco idea I ever heard tell of! Why'd she want to come to this place?"

Longarm shook his head. "I don't know. The conversation never got that far, because I turned her down flat."

McCready snorted. "I should hope to smile you would."

"The marshal in Brimstone told me that she's been around there for a month or so, trying to find someone to bring her out here. I guess when I turned her down, it was the last straw and she decided to set out on her own."

"Then she lost her horse in that sandstorm, just like you did, I reckon."

"More than likely," said Longarm. Maybe there was more to the story than that, maybe not. They could find out once they had revived Melinda Kelly.

He carried her into the trading post and gently placed her on the counter where he had slept the night before. It didn't have too much sand on it. She lay there, still sense-less, but she was murmuring something now, which told Longarm she was closer to regaining consciousness. He asked McCready, "Can you fetch a bucket of water?"

"Sure. Be right back."

McCready hurried off. Longarm undid the top button on Melinda's shirt so she could breathe easier. That was really the reason, too, he told himself. He was too much of a gentleman to be trying to sneak a peak at the breasts of an unconscious lady . . . no matter how nice they mounded there under her shirt.

When McCready came back with the bucket, Longarm scooped up some water in his right hand and eased his left behind Melinda's neck so he could lift her head. Her lips parted a little. He dribbled the water from his cupped hand into her mouth. Her tongue came out, acting on its own instincts, and licked greedily at the moisture that spilled outside her mouth.

Longarm gave her more water, but some of this must have gone down the wrong way. Melinda started to choke and cough. As the spasms shook her, Longarm lifted her into a sitting position and slapped her lightly on the back, trying to help clear her throat.

Suddenly, she let out a scream and started flailing around, throwing wild punches. One of her fists thudded into Longarm's bare chest but didn't do any damage. He put his hands on her shoulders and began to shake her, saying, "Miss Kelly! Miss Kelly! Melinda! Settle down! Everything's all right!"

Everything was a far cry from all right, he thought, but she didn't have to know that right now. It would be better if she calmed down first, before he broke the news of the bad fix they were in.

Slowly, she stopped hitting at him. Her terrified screams died away. Her eyes opened, and she stared at him, first in total incomprehension, but then gradually with dawning understanding.

"Marshal? Marshal Long?" she asked in a half whisper. "Wh-where are we? And . . . and why are you . . . ," her voice dropped even more, *"naked?"*

"What?" asked Longarm, thrown for a loop by the question. Then he realized that standing beside the counter like he was, she couldn't see the lower half of his body all that well. She had seen his bare chest and assumed that he was bare all the way down to the ground, he supposed.

He stepped back so that she could get a better look at him and said, "No offense, Miss Kelly, but I ain't naked. Just had to make a rope out of my shirt."

"A . . . rope?"

Longarm waved that off. "It's a long story." He nodded toward his companion. "This is Deputy Sheriff Haygood McCready."

McCready snatched his old hat off and said, "I'm mighty pleased and honored to make your acquaintance, ma'am." He held the bucket out with his other hand. "Would you like some more water?"

"Oh, God, yes!" Melinda exclaimed. She grabbed the bucket and lifted it to her mouth, drinking so thirstily that she spilled some of the water. It ran down the smooth skin of her throat and trickled into the valley between her breasts. Longarm couldn't help but notice.

He wasn't so distracted that he couldn't think straight, though. He reached out, took hold of the bucket, and gently but firmly pulled it away from her. Melinda cried, "Wait! I wasn't through!"

"Guzzle down too much, too fast, and it'll just make you sick," he told her. "We've got plenty of water, but you want to keep down what you've already drank."

She sighed. "I suppose you're right. I just . . . I was never so thirsty in all my life. All this sand, and that terrible sun . . ."

"Yeah, it'll dry a fella out in a hurry," said Longarm. "A gal, too. Wait a couple of minutes, and you can drink some more. Until then, why don't you tell me and Deputy McCready how you happened to show up out here. I reckon you decided to try to find Abaddon by yourself?"

"Not by myself," she snapped. "My wagons finally showed up yesterday. I was beginning to think they had gotten lost and would never reach Brimstone."

"Wait a minute," Longarm said. "Wagons?"

"That's right. I hired some wagons and drivers in San Antonio, and I was supposed to meet them in Brimstone two weeks ago. By that time, I expected to have hired someone to help me find this place . . ." She frowned at Longarm. "But you saw how well that worked out."

"So when they turned up, you headed out into the desert without a guide?" said Longarm.

McCready added, "With a big ol' sandstorm comin'?"

"Well, I didn't *know* there was a sandstorm coming, now did I?" Melinda snapped. "Didn't it catch the two of you out here?"

McCready scratched his jaw. "Reckon she's got us there, Marshal."

"Where are the wagons now?" asked Longarm. "What were you doing walking across the desert by yourself?"

"When that storm hit, the man who's in charge of the wagon train said we needed to hunker down and wait it out. Unfortunately, I was on horseback, and my mount got spooked and ran away. Then I fell off, and . . . and . . ." A shudder ran through her, and she put her hands over her face for a moment. "I don't want to talk about it," she said, her voice muffled. "I don't even want to think about it, ever again. It . . . it was the most horrible experience I've ever gone through."

"You made it through the storm, though," said McCready. "That's sayin' somethin', ma'am. A lot of folks would've just give up and laid down to die."

Melinda's chin lifted defiantly. "I don't believe in giving up when I want something. And I wanted to live."

Longarm said, "You wanted to find this settlement, too."

"That's right. So when the sun rose this morning, I put my back to it and started walking. I knew I was going in the right general direction, so I trusted to luck." She smiled. "And I was lucky. You found me, Marshal Long."

"Deputy McCready's the one who spotted you first," said Longarm, which made McCready grin and preen a little. "I just went out and brought you in."

"Thank you. I hadn't had any water since yesterday afternoon, and I . . . I really didn't know how much longer I could keep on going." She looked around the room. "Do you have anything to eat? I'm really hungry, too."

"Well, now, that's a mite of a problem," the deputy sheriff said. "The marshal and me lost all our supplies when our mounts run off, just like yours did."

Melinda's eyes widened. "So you don't have any food?"

"Nary a bite."

"But we'll all starve!"

"Maybe not," said Longarm. "You said your wagons are still out there somewhere. What sort of teams were pulling them?"

"Oxen."

Longarm nodded. "An ox won't get all skittish and bolt like a horse or a mule. Chances are, the wagons and the teams made it through the storm all right. Will your drivers push on, even though you're missing?"

She frowned in thought. "I don't really know. You don't think they'd just turn around and go back to Brimstone, do you?"

"Let's hope not," Longarm replied with a grim smile. "Them finding Abaddon is the best chance we have for getting out of this alive."

"Sure enough," McCready agreed. "They'll have food and water, and they can fill their barrels at the well here afore we start back to Brimstone."

"The well?" Melinda repeated. "I thought the well was covered with sand."

"It was." McCready grinned. "The marshal and me, we dug it out!"

"Can I see?" Melinda asked with surprising eagerness in her voice.

Longarm nodded. "Sure. We can show you around the settlement, what there is of it. You went to so much trouble to get out here, I reckon you deserve to have a look at it."

He put his hands under her arms and lifted her down from the counter, and as he did so he was aware of the warm pressure of her rounded breasts against his bare forearms. Melinda seemed to notice the contact, too, because she lowered her eyes and he thought he saw a blush steal faintly over her face.

Longarm let go of her and stepped back. "We're pretty sure this was your grandfather's trading post," he said. "It must be, because it's the biggest building in town, and it's got another wing on the side where he added on a saloon."

"And a brothel," she said. "You don't have to shield me from the truth about my grandfather, Marshal Long. I know about his various business enterprises."

"Well, then, uh, this is it." Longarm waved a hand at their surroundings. "There's a blacksmith shop across the street, as well as several other buildings. We don't know what was in them, though."

"I'd like to take a look around anyway."

"Sure. Come on." He ushered her toward the front door, and as she walked past him, he saw her cut her eyes toward his bare chest with what seemed like considerable interest. Even in what might be dire circumstances, it was difficult for men and women to ignore the natural urges they felt toward each other, he thought.

As they walked outside, he said, "Just what was it that made you want to bring some wagons all the way out here, Miss Kelly?"

"No offense, Marshal, and I don't want you to think that I'm ungrateful since you did carry me in from the desert . . . but that's my business. Family business."

"I'm just curious, that's all," said Longarm. "I've looked all over this place, and there ain't that much to see. I'm danged if I can figure out what anybody might find here that would need wagons to carry it away."

"Like I said—"

Longarm held up a hand to stop her. "None of my business, I know. I reckon that when you're a lawman, you get in the habit of poking into things. Ain't that right, Deputy McCready?"

The old-timer had followed them out of the trading post. McCready seemed not to notice the question at first, then he said, "What? Oh. Yeah. Lawman. Pokin' into things. It's a habit, all right." He paused, then asked the young woman, "Did you see my signal flashes from the top o' the buildin'?"

"I did," Melinda replied. "And thank goodness I did, because they gave me something to aim at and a reason to keep going. When I saw them, I thought that maybe someone else was out here. Of course, I was hoping you'd have horses . . ."

Longarm didn't mention the three outlaws. Now he had more reason than ever to hope that Garth, Thompson, and Dumont would show up and have all three of their horses with them. He and McCready and Melinda would need those animals to get back to Brimstone.

It didn't take long for the two lawmen to show Melinda around Abaddon. She was especially interested in the well, putting her hands on the wall and leaning over to peer down into the water, which had risen to within a few feet of the top. The sand had settled, too, as Longarm had thought it would, and at least on top, the water was clear and inviting.

Melinda must have felt the same way, because she

said, "I'd love to take my clothes off and jump in there so I could wash all this blasted sand off of me." Then she blushed again as she realized what she'd said.

McCready opened his mouth to make some comment, but Longarm caught his eye and gave him a hard look. Longarm figured McCready was thinking the same thing he was. He'd love to see Melinda splashing around in that water, too. McCready might be old, but he wasn't dead yet.

After a moment, Melinda asked, "What do you think the chances are that the wagons will find this place?"

"Do you have a good wagon master?" asked Longarm.

"Mr. Barstow is supposed to be one of the best at that sort of work."

"If it was me, I'd send some riders to look for you— the wagons *did* have outriders to serve as scouts?"

Melinda nodded. "Yes, three men."

"Then I'd send those hombres to look for you," Longarm went on, "while I got the wagons rolling and kept heading west. This fella Barstow has to figure that if you survived the storm, you'd try to make it to Abaddon."

"I made it clear that I had every intention of getting here, yes. It's reasonable to expect that he'd think I'd head in this direction."

Longarm spread his hands. "There you go. All we have to do is wait for the wagons to show up. I reckon you brought plenty of supplies with you?"

She nodded again. "Yes, of course. We have enough provisions for a couple of weeks."

McCready said, "Even with a couple o' extra mouths to feed in me and the marshal, that ought to be enough to get us back to Brimstone with plenty to spare." He held up the piece of mirror. "I'm gonna climb back on the roof and go to signalin' again. Maybe that'll help them wagons find us."

Longarm thought that was a good idea. He gave McCready a hand getting onto the roof, then said to Melinda, "You'd better go back inside, out of the sun. It'll just get more fierce as the day goes on."

"Thank you." She frowned suddenly. "What happened to my hat?"

Longarm returned the frown. "Your hat? Why, I reckon it's still out there on the desert where you passed out. I just picked you up and didn't think to get your hat, too."

"I'd really like to have it back. I should go get it."

She turned and started toward the edge of the settlement. Longarm reached out and put a hand on her arm to stop her.

"I'll fetch your hat for you, Miss Kelly," he told her.

Her frown went away, to be replaced by a dazzling smile. "That's very kind of you, Marshal Long. But if you're going to be doing favors for me, don't you think you ought to call me Melinda?"

"I'd be mighty happy to, as long as you call me Custis."

"I think I can do that. And I can come with you if you like . . ."

Longarm shook his head. "No need for that. You can satisfy my curiosity, though. What's so special about this hat?"

"Nothing really, I suppose," she said. "It belonged to my grandfather, that's all. I brought it with me when I came out here because I felt it was somehow like . . . having him here with me, I guess you could say."

"I understand. Go on inside now, and get out of the sun. I'll be back in a few minutes."

Melinda went into the trading post. Longarm stepped out into the street and looked up at the roof, where McCready was using the broken mirror to flash signals to whoever might see them.

"Haygood!" Longarm called. "I'm gonna get the lady's hat that I left out in the desert!"

McCready looked down at him. "What?"

"Hat!" Longarm pointed at his head. "Hat!"

"You can't have my hat! I need it. I'm sorry you lost yours, but this here's my hat."

Longarm shook his head and held up a hand, palm out. "Never mind." He turned and started out of Abaddon, toward the place where he had found Melinda Kelly.

As he trudged through the sand, he tried to remember when his hat had blown away. He knew it was sometime during the storm, but he couldn't recall exactly when. Not that it mattered, of course. McCready had jammed his battered old hat down tight on his head, and held on to it, too, but Longarm had been busy trying to lead the horse.

He could understand somebody having a sentimental attachment to a grandfather's hat, he supposed. He had been through dozens of the flat-crowned, snuff-brown Stetsons he favored, but none of them had belonged to his old grandpappy.

After a few minutes, he spotted Melinda's brown hat lying on the ground. The wind was light at the moment, so it hadn't blown away. He went over and picked it up, turned it over in his hands. He could tell now that it was old. Before, he hadn't paid much attention to it. He'd been too surprised to find Melinda out here in the middle of the desert. It was just a plain hat, a little fancier than some because it had a lining. That lining had come loose in one place, showing its age.

Longarm started back toward the settlement. He hadn't gone very far when he noticed McCready waving his arms over his head, as if he were trying to get Longarm's attention. Even though hunger and weariness gripped him and the sun was getting mighty hot again, the big lawman broke into a trot, swinging the hat he'd recovered at his side.

When he was close enough, he stopped and cupped his hands around his mouth. "Haygood!" he shouted. "What is it?"

McCready was practically jumping up and down in excitement. He pointed off to the east and yelled back the words Longarm wanted to hear.

"The wagons! I can see the wagons! They're comin'!"

Chapter 8

Longarm loped on into town. By the time he reached the trading post, McCready had climbed down from the roof, and he and Melinda stood on the porch, waiting.

"How many wagons did you see?" asked Longarm.

"Three."

"And that's how many I brought with me," said Melinda. "I'm sure they're my wagons. Mr. Barstow pushed on just the way I expected he would."

"Somebody flashed back at me, so I know they saw my signals," McCready added with a big grin. "Looks like we ain't a-gonna starve to death after all."

Melinda looked at the old hat in Longarm's hand and said, "You found my grandfather's hat!"

"Sure," he said as he handed it to her. "It was right where I thought it would be. You were lucky the wind's not blowing very hard, so it hadn't gone sailing off like it would have yesterday. You must've hung on to it mighty tight to keep it from blowing away during that storm."

She nodded, then settled the hat on her head. "It's all I

have left of my grandfather. Well, it and this town. Of course I hung on to it."

Longarm began to wonder if she was planning to claim Abaddon as her own. He didn't know if William O'Sullivan had had any other heirs. Of course, as she had pointed out a couple of times, it wasn't really any of his business, but there was no law against wondering, was there?

If she did intend to claim the settlement, he didn't have any earthly idea why she would do such a thing. Abaddon had been a failure. It was just a ghost town now, of no value to anybody.

They stood there in the shade of the porch and watched, and in a few minutes, the wagons came into sight, rolling steadily toward the buildings. The canvas-covered vehicles rocked a little as their wheels passed over humps in the sand. The massive, stolid oxen pulling the wagons didn't get in any hurry, so it took a while for them to reach the town.

When they did, Melinda ran forward to meet them. Longarm saw the man on the driver's seat of the lead wagon grin and lift a hand in greeting. He was obviously happy to see Melinda.

Longarm and McCready walked out into the street at a slower pace. The driver of the lead wagon brought his team to a halt and jumped down from the box.

"Miss Kelly!" he said. "It's mighty good to see you again. I was afraid you'd gotten lost in that sandstorm."

"I did," said Melinda as she came up to him. "My horse threw me and ran off. But I managed to make it through the night, and then this morning I walked on until I came to Abaddon."

The man looked around at the old buildings. "This is it, then? The place you were looking for?"

"That's right, Mr. Barstow. This is Abaddon. That was my grandfather's trading post."

Barstow looked at Longarm and McCready, his eyes narrowing with suspicion as he did so. He nodded toward them and asked, "Who are the cowboy and the desert rat?"

McCready bristled. "Desert rat? Who're you callin' a desert rat, mister? I ain't no desert rat!"

"Take it easy, Haygood," said Longarm. To Barstow, he went on, "I ain't a cowboy, either, although I done my share of punching cattle when I was younger. As it happens, we're both lawmen. I'm Deputy U.S. Marshal Custis Long, and this is Deputy Sheriff Haygood McCready, from Crockett County."

Barstow grunted. He was a barrel-chested man with gray hair under his pushed-back black Stetson. "Pleased to meet you, Marshal," he said. "I got to admit, I'm wondering what you and Deputy McCready are doing out here."

"Saving my life," Melinda said with a smile. "I followed Deputy McCready's signal flashes toward Abaddon, and when I passed out from thirst before I got here, Marshal Long retrieved me from the desert. They dug out my grandfather's old well, too, and it's full of water."

That news put a grin on Barstow's face. "I'm mighty glad to hear that. We've got water in the barrels, but you can't ever have enough in a damned desert like this. Pardon my French, ma'am."

Melinda nodded. Her tone was brisk and businesslike as she went on, "We'll stay here today, let the oxen rest, and top off those water barrels. Then we'll start back to Brimstone in the morning."

"Yes, ma'am," said Barstow, with the air of a man who knew who was paying the bills.

"You or one of those other drivers wouldn't happen to have a spare shirt among your supplies, would you?" asked Longarm.

Barstow rubbed his jaw and considered for a moment before nodding. "I reckon we can come up with something for you to wear, Marshal. What happened to your shirt?"

"We had to tear it up to make a rope, so we could lower a bucket up and down in the well."

"Sounds like a good reason to me." Barstow turned and waved to the other drivers. "Get down and unhitch your teams, boys! We'll be staying here today and starting back in the morning."

The men nodded their understanding and got busy following the wagon master's orders.

Longarm said, "Miss Kelly told me you have some outriders with the wagons. Where are they?"

Barstow nodded toward the young woman. "Out looking for Miss Kelly. But I told them to work their way back in this direction, so they ought to be showing up after a while."

"I can go back up on the roof and keep signalin' with this here busted mirror," McCready offered. "Might help 'em find the place easier."

"That's a good idea, thanks."

McCready rubbed his chin. "I could do with a bite to eat first, though."

"Yes," Melinda said eagerly. "I think we all could."

Barstow waved toward the rear of the wagon. "Help yourself to the supplies. We've got plenty of provisions."

That proved to be true. Using broken wood from the buildings, they soon had a campfire going. One of the men cooked bacon and biscuits and brewed a pot of coffee. While that was going on, Barstow found a spare shirt for Longarm. It was a little short in the sleeves and tight across the shoulders, but it was better than nothing. There wasn't an extra hat in the wagons, but Longarm figured he'd just stay in the shade as much as possible.

Being fully dressed and having his belly filled with food went a long way toward making him feel like himself again. It also made him sleepy. He went into the trading post, figuring that he'd stretch out on one of the counters and maybe take a nap.

He found Melinda there, holding her grandfather's hat in her hands and gazing into it. She looked a little embarrassed when Longarm found her and clapped the hat on her head again.

He smiled. "Thinking about your granddad?"

"That's right. This place was a dream of his. He wanted to build something he could call his own. It's a shame that it never quite worked out."

"Yeah, I reckon. Most folks never get their dreams, though, and even those who do find out about half the time that it wasn't what they really wanted after all."

She moved closer to him and smiled. "I didn't realize that you were a philosopher as well as a lawman, Custis."

Longarm shook his head. "Just talking, not philosophizing. I'm a simple hombre. I don't think deep thoughts."

"I'm not sure I believe that." She was standing fairly close to him now, her head tipped back slightly so that she could look up into his eyes. "I'll tell you one deep thought I had earlier, though."

"All right."

"I was a little disappointed when Mr. Barstow found that shirt for you. I was . . . enjoying looking at that chest of yours."

Longarm smiled. "I reckon I'm glad you found the view to your liking."

"Oh, yes, very much to my liking." Her tongue came out and played swiftly over her lips. "Would you care to have a look at my chest?"

Longarm glanced toward the door. He and Melinda were alone in the trading post. McCready was up on the roof, signaling again, and the men who'd come with the wagons were all outside, busy with various chores.

"I wouldn't mind," he said.

With a mischievous smile on her face, Melinda lifted her hands to the buttons of the man's shirt she wore and began undoing them. She spread the shirt open, revealing her breasts. The pale globes of female flesh weren't all that big, but they were as firm and pert as ripe apples. Her small, pink nipples were growing hard.

Longarm brought his hands up and cupped her breasts. He stroked her nipples with his thumbs and brought them to an even tighter state of erection. Melinda's eyes grew heavy-lidded, and a sigh of pleasure came from her parted lips.

"Suck on them," she said with a note of urgency in her voice.

Longarm obliged her, bending over to suck first one nipple, then the other, into his mouth. His lips closed over them in turn, and his tongue swirled around them as he continued to knead and caress her breasts. Melinda sighed again and ran her fingers through his hair as his skilled efforts brought her to a higher pitch of arousal.

After a couple of minutes, Longarm lifted his mouth. With a soft growl of desire, he put his arms around her waist and pulled her against him. His mouth came down on hers in an urgent kiss. Her lips were already parted and offered no resistance as his tongue slid between them into the hot, wet cavern of her mouth. She met it eagerly with her tongue, which danced around his. Her breasts were flattened against his chest, and he felt those hard nipples prodding his skin through the shirt he wore.

He was hard now, almost painfully erect inside his denim trousers. Melinda rubbed her pelvis against his stiff pecker, grunting and moaning as she humped into him. Both of them were hot and horny as hell, and Longarm was tempted to pick her up, set her on the counter, and pull enough clothes off of both of them so that he could drive his shaft into her.

Some of the others could walk into the trading post at any moment, though, and he knew it. He wasn't what you'd call a bashful hombre, not by any stretch of the imagination, but he didn't want anything to embarrass Melinda or make her uncomfortable.

So he reluctantly lifted his mouth away from hers and said, a little breathless, "I reckon it'd be better if we waited until we can have a little more privacy."

She was breathless, too. "I . . . I . . ." She sighed. "You're right. I know you're right, Custis." She leaned forward and ran the tip of her tongue over his lips. "But it's awfully hard to stop."

"It'll be even better later."

"I'll hold you to that promise!" She reached between them and squeezed his manhood through his trousers to emphasize her words. "Tonight, after everyone's gone to sleep?"

Longarm planned to see to it that someone stood guard again all night, but whoever had sentry duty would probably be outside.

"Barstow and his men will likely sleep in the wagons," he said. "Give it a while after everybody's turned in, and then we'll meet in here."

"All right." She giggled. "I'll be discreet."

"Good idea."

"Waiting like this is going to make for a long day, Custis." She squeezed him again. "Long and hard."

He had to close his eyes and blow out a breath as her touch sent throbs of pleasure through him. "I don't reckon truer words were ever spoken," he said.

Melinda's prediction proved to be true. With him having a pretty good idea what was waiting for him that night, the day passed with agonizing slowness for Longarm. But he borrowed a blanket from one of the wagons, folded it up to use as a pillow, and spent quite a bit of the time sleeping on the counter in the trading post. He also drank a couple of buckets of water and had two more good meals from the supplies the wagons had brought with them, so by evening he felt that he had recovered for the most part from the ordeal he had gone through.

That was probably a good thing, he thought, because if Melinda was as lithe and eager as she appeared to be, he was going to need all the strength he could get.

The outriders who had been searching for Melinda rode into Abaddon late that afternoon and were relieved to find that she was already there. After everyone had eaten supper, Longarm got together with McCready and Barstow and discussed setting up guard shifts.

The first thing Barstow wanted to know was why they needed sentries. "As far as I can tell, we're the only ones out here in this wasteland," he said.

"That may not be true," Longarm explained. "Before that sandstorm hit, Deputy McCready and I were after some outlaws who tried to cross the desert after a little ruckus I had with them in Brimstone. There are three of them, or at least there were when they rode into the desert, and they're all cold-blooded killers."

"You really think they're wandering around out here somewhere, after that storm yesterday?"

"Haygood and I made it through the storm, and so did Miss Kelly. We don't have any way of knowing what happened to those owlhoots. But if they *are* alive, and if they happened to stumble into this place, they'd like nothing better than to kill us all and take those wagons and supplies."

Actually, they probably wouldn't kill Melinda right away, thought Longarm . . . but she would probably wish that they had by the time they got through with her.

Barstow scratched at his jaw as he thought, then after a moment he nodded and said, "Yeah, I reckon it'd be a good idea to post some guards, all right. There are eight of us, not counting Miss Kelly. Should we split up the night into four two-man shifts?"

"Sounds like a right smart plan," said McCready. "That way nobody has to lose more'n a couple of hours o' sleep."

Longarm agreed. He volunteered to take the last shift. That would give him plenty of time with Melinda, and time to get some sleep, too . . . depending on just how eager she really was.

They agreed that a guard would be posted at each end of town. Barstow's men were well armed with rifles and pistols, and Longarm and McCready would each borrow a Winchester when it was their turn to stand guard. McCready planned to sleep under one of the wagons, making a bedroll out of borrowed blankets.

"These bones o' mine are too old and brittle to spend another night on a bar," he said. "I reckon that sandy ground'll be a mite softer."

Longarm didn't see Melinda before everyone turned

in, but he was confident that she hadn't forgotten about their rendezvous.

Still using the folded-up blanket as a pillow, he stretched out on the counter in the darkness and waited. He dozed a little, but he slept lightly enough so that he woke at the first sound of a soft footstep at the door of the trading post.

He sat up, heard the footsteps stealing closer, and eased his hand over to the butt of his Colt, just in case the person moving quietly across the room turned out not to be Melinda Kelly.

He didn't have to worry about that. She whispered, "Custis?"

"Right here," he whispered back. She came into his arms, and despite the darkness, their mouths instinctively found each other.

Her kiss was as hot and hungry now as it had been earlier. As their lips pressed together, Longarm unbuttoned her shirt and cupped her breasts again. Melinda clutched at his shoulders and kissed him that much harder.

After a moment, she pulled back and said, "Even though you infuriated me when we first met, Custis, I wanted you then . . . and I still do."

"You told me you were a lady who went after what you wanted."

She reached for the buttons of his trousers. "I certainly am."

He unbuckled his gunbelt, coiled it, and set it aside where it would be within easy reach if he should happen to need the Colt. Melinda finished unfastening his trousers, and he lifted his hips from the counter so that she could slide them down, along with the bottom half of a pair of long underwear.

Freed of those tight confines, his shaft sprang free, jutting up from his groin like a bar of iron. Melinda wrapped her soft hands around it, or tried to, anyway. Her fingers didn't quite reach.

"My God, Custis," she breathed. "I never felt one so big before." Even though he couldn't see the flush that must have spread across her face, he heard the sudden embarrassment in her voice as she added, "Not that I've, ah, felt all that many, uh, male members . . ."

"Don't worry about that," he told her. "As far as I'm concerned, all I care about is what we're doing right here and now."

"I feel the same way." She ran a fingertip around the silky crown of his manhood. "Would you mind terribly if I . . . found out just how much of this I can fit in my mouth? I know it's terribly brazen of me—"

"That'd be fine," Longarm assured her. He knew she was just teasing him, anyway. You'd have to search for a long time, maybe forever, to find an hombre who *would* mind something like that.

He was sitting on the edge of the counter, which meant Melinda didn't have to bend very far as she moved between his thighs and leaned over to kiss and lick the head of his cock. Longarm sighed in pleasure as her warm lips and tongue tantalized him.

After a moment or two of that exquisite torment, she opened her lips wide and took the head inside her mouth. She was able to slide her mouth a couple more inches down the shaft, but that was all. She began to suck gently as Longarm caressed her bare breasts.

What she was doing to him felt so good that he could have spent himself right then and there, filling her mouth with his juices. He controlled the urge, even though it got mighty difficult to do so when she cupped his heavy balls in one delicate little hand and rolled them back and forth. He just about shot off when she did that.

After a few minutes of that exquisite torment, Longarm put his hands on her face and lifted her mouth away from his shaft. He moved his hands under her arms and picked her up effortlessly, setting her on top of the counter with him. As quickly as she could, she peeled off her trousers, then, still wearing the open shirt, she straddled him and poised her hips above his throbbing member.

"Careful, Custis," she said. "I've never had one so big inside me before."

He held her hips to steady her as she grabbed his cock with one hand and guided the tip of it to the already drenched opening between her legs. As wet and aroused as she was, the head slipped easily between the fleshy folds of her sex.

It felt so good, Longarm couldn't help but move his hips a little, penetrating deeper into her, but for the most part, he lay back and allowed her to set the pace. Slowly, deliciously, maddeningly, she lowered herself onto him, filling herself with his rock-hard manhood.

Finally, nearly all of his shaft was sheathed within her. When she was unable to take any more, she braced her hands on his broad, hairy chest and began to pump her hips back and forth. Longarm timed his thrusts to match hers, sliding in and out of her slowly and gently at first.

But as the moments went by, his pace became harder and faster, and so did hers. Mingled passion and lust rose within them and became pure, driving desire. Longarm's eyes had adjusted well enough to the darkness that he could see the slight bobbing of her breasts as she rode him. That lured his hands to them. He squeezed them and thumbed the hard nipples. Melinda made a little panting sound in her throat as her pace increased to a gallop.

Finally she threw her head back and let out a long, shuddery sigh as spasms rippled through her. Longarm felt those spasms as her interior muscles clutched at him, and that set off his own climax. He drove up into her as deeply as he could and began to empty himself, spurt after throbbing spurt that filled her to overflowing with his essence.

When it was over, Melinda sagged forward and rested her head on his chest. Longarm stroked her long, dark hair and felt the tiny trembles that still shook her inside. He felt her heart as well, slugging heavily against his chest.

"Custis, that . . . that was . . . magnificent," she said when she had caught her breath enough that she could talk again. "I . . . I never experienced anything like that before!"

"Always happy to oblige a lady," murmured Longarm.

"Well, you obliged me, that's for sure!" Melinda said with a happy laugh. She wiggled her hips. He was still partially erect inside her, and that made delicious sensations go through both of them. "What I want to know now is . . . how soon can you do it again?"

Yeah, thought Longarm, he was mighty glad he had gotten most of his strength back.

Chapter 9

It was late when Melinda slipped out of the trading post and went back to the wagon where she was supposed to sleep. Longarm hoped for her sake that none of the men spotted her, but he wasn't sure she would really care all that much if they did. As she had said, she was a young woman accustomed to getting her own way, and she struck him as the sort who wouldn't lose any sleep over what other people thought of her.

He was able to get a few hours of slumber himself before instinct woke him and told him it was time for him to take his turn on guard. He was paired with Barstow. McCready was taking the shift just before Longarm, along with one of the other drivers.

Longarm left the trading post and walked toward the end of town where McCready was supposed to be standing guard. He called softly, "Haygood!"

When McCready responded, it was from behind Longarm, which came as something of a surprise to the big lawman. "Marshal?" the deputy sheriff said. "Is that you?"

Longarm turned and saw McCready emerging from the building that had housed the blacksmith shop years earlier. "What were you doing in there?" Longarm asked with a nod toward the building. "Hear something suspicious?"

"In there? Naw. I was just, uh, answerin' the call o' nature."

"Oh," said Longarm. He wasn't sure why McCready couldn't have waited until his turn at guard duty was over . . . but then, he wasn't as old as McCready was, either. "Any problems out here?"

"Nary a one. Been as quiet as a whorehouse on a Sunday mornin'. Is it time for you to take over?"

"Yeah."

"I'll go get a mite more shut-eye, then." McCready handed over the Winchester he was carrying, then hesitated. "Marshal, there's somethin' I been wonderin' about."

"What's that?" asked Longarm.

"Them owlhoots we was both a-chasin' . . . you plan to go after 'em again, once you get back to Brimstone?"

"Billy Vail sent me to track them down. Until they're behind bars, or I know they're dead, my job's not done."

McCready waved a gnarled hand at the desert. "But they could be anywheres out yonder in that sand! You might search for a year and never find their carcasses. Now, I'm as devoted to the law as the next badge toter, Marshal, but I'm goin' back to Crockett County and tellin' the sheriff them varmints is either long gone or buzzard bait. I think you ought to tell your boss the same."

Longarm shook his head. "I appreciate what you're saying, Haygood, but I have to at least try to find them. I can't search this desert all the way from one end to the other, I suppose, but I plan to outfit myself in Brimstone and have a good look through the center of it, where O'Sullivan's old road ran. That's what I started out to do, and I plan to finish that part of the job, anyway."

McCready took his hat off and scratched his head. "Well, I reckon you're just about the stubbornest galoot I ever did see, then. Ain't nobody else'd go to that much trouble."

"That's just the way I see things," Longarm said with a shrug.

"Well, it's your business, I reckon."

With that, McCready walked off toward the wagons. Longarm tucked the rifle under his arm and strolled to the western edge of the settlement. He leaned against the last building in that direction and looked out over the desert. The moon floated low above it, casting a shimmering silver light on the sand. Back to the east, a band of gray along the horizon signified the approach of dawn.

Longarm wondered what dawn would bring. He didn't believe that Melinda would return to Brimstone without whatever it was that had brought her out here in the first place. Despite her reluctance to admit what that was, she was going to have to reveal her secret before they could start back. Abaddon was too small to hide very much.

The rest of the night passed quietly. Barstow and his men were up before the sun, tending to the oxen and preparing breakfast. Longarm walked over to the wagons, nodded to Barstow, and said, "Morning."

"Any trouble last night on your end of town?" asked the wagon master.

Longarm shook his head and replied, "Not a bit, as far as I know."

"Yeah, that's what my men reported, too. Like I said last night, we're the only ones out here. The only ones alive, anyway."

"You're probably right," said Longarm. "Where's Miss Kelly?"

Barstow pointed with a thumb toward the third wagon. "Still asleep, I think. I was about to go wake her up for breakfast."

"I'll do that," Longarm offered. He was curious whether Melinda would look as good when she first woke up as she did the rest of the time. He was willing to bet a hat that she did. At least, he would have been if he still *had* a hat.

He walked to the last wagon in line, passing the second one, where Haygood McCready snored raucously from a bedroll underneath the vehicle. Longarm went to the back of the wagon where Melinda was sleeping and paused at the canvas flap that covered the opening. He listened to see if she was already moving around in there. Not hearing anything, he lifted a corner of the flap.

She lay there on a pile of blankets, sleeping peacefully with her face turned toward him, and even in the dim light, Longarm thought she was lovely. Her grandfather's hat lay beside her, upside down. Longarm glanced at it, then looked again, a slight frown creasing his forehead.

The lining inside the hat was torn, and he saw something peeking out from underneath it. A corner of a piece of paper, he thought, but he couldn't be sure. Idly curious, he reached over the wagon's tailgate and picked up the hat.

There was definitely a piece of paper stuck up inside the lining. He wondered if Melinda knew about it. Maybe that was why she had been so insistent that she had to get the hat back the day before. Still frowning, Longarm slipped the paper out through the torn place.

It had been folded several times. He felt a little bad about poking into Melinda's private business, but like he had told her, it was a lawman's habit to find answers to questions. Anyway, she was going to have to reveal what she was after soon enough.

He unfolded the paper.

The squares and lines drawn on it, along with the arrow marked "N," told him right away that it was a map. And it didn't take but a second for him to study the layout of the buildings and realize that it was a map of Abaddon. There was the trading post, and a circle at the eastern end of it marked the location of the well.

A broken line led north from the well, and scrawled next to it was the number "50." Was that supposed to be fifty yards, fifty feet, fifty paces? Longarm didn't know.

But at the end of that line was a big letter "X."

In storybooks, the place where pirates buried their treasure was always marked on maps with an X. Longarm didn't know how much truth there was to those pirate stories, but from the looks of this map, something was buried out there, north of the well. Judging by the creases in the paper and the way the ink had faded, the map was pretty old. He had a hunch it had been drawn by William O'Sullivan, the dreamer who had dug the well and founded Abaddon.

He had a hunch as well that whatever was out there, it was what had brought Melinda Kelly to the desert.

He was about to turn around, wake her, and ask her about it when he heard a sound he knew all too well: the metallic ratcheting of a gun being cocked.

"Damn it, Custis," she said. "Why couldn't you just

stop trying to find out what I was doing out here?"

He looked over his shoulder at her, saw that she had pushed herself up on one elbow. She had a small-caliber pistol in her other hand, pointed straight at him. The gun was rock-steady in her grip.

"You were gonna have to dig it up, whatever it is, before you started back to Brimstone," he said. "I would have found out then what was going on."

She sat up and shook her head. "No. I was going to make another trip later, after you and Mr. McCready had gone on about your business. That way neither of you would have ever known what this was all about."

"What *is* it all about?" asked Longarm, still without turning around. "Must be something illegal, or else you wouldn't have been trying to keep it hidden from a couple of lawmen." He lifted the map he had taken from its hiding place in the lining of O'Sullivan's hat. "Buried loot of some sort would be my guess."

"And it would be a good one," Melinda admitted. "You see, Custis, my grandfather wasn't just a businessman who ran a trading post and tried to start a town."

"Then he must have been some sort of owlhoot."

"He was a man who knew what he wanted." She paused. "I suppose I inherited that quality from him. And he wanted to be a rich man . . . whatever it took to achieve that." She took a deep breath, then went on. "He put in the wagon road and the trading post to draw the wagon trains through the desert. Then, after they had stopped here to take on water, he . . . he and the men who worked for him waited until the wagons had started on west and . . ."

She stopped as if she couldn't force herself to go on.

Longarm put the rest of it together in his mind without

too much trouble. He had been around enough ruthless outlaws to know how they operated.

"Then they ambushed those pilgrims out in the desert and murdered them," he said in a hard, flat voice. "Your grandfather killed them and stole everything they had that was worth anything, and eventually the sand covered up the evidence of what he'd done."

"Not . . . all of them," she said. "He let some of the wagon trains go on through without ever bothering them."

Longarm nodded. "Yeah, he'd do that, all right. If every bunch of immigrants that started through the desert disappeared, pretty soon the wagon trains would stop using that trail, no matter how many days it saved them. He probably just hit the trains that had quite a bit of money with them. Some of those groups pooled all their cash and had a good-sized nest egg to help them get started on their new lives when they got to where they were going." His voice hardened again. "Until your grandfather snuffed 'em out, so they didn't have any lives at all."

"You can't blame me for that," Melinda said between clenched teeth. "I was just a baby at the time."

"How'd you find out about it?" Longarm kept watching the gun in Melinda's hand. So far, it wasn't shaking any. But if he kept her talking, her hand might start to tremble. He might have a chance to knock the pistol aside and take it away from her.

"When he had enough saved up, he buried all the money and the jewelry out there in the sand and then left Abaddon. Everyone else left, too. It never would have lasted as an actual town, anyway. He just couldn't keep the well going because the sandstorms kept clogging it up. After that happened, he went back home to Ohio, where I was born and raised."

"Why didn't he just take the loot with him?"

"He didn't want anybody suspecting what he'd done. He thought that if he showed up back home with a lot of money, people would wonder where it came from. He was worried about the jewelry he had, too. He thought if he tried to sell it, somebody might trace it back to its original owners. Since everything was safe where he had buried it, he was going to wait a few years, then come back and dig it up, and then he'd take the rest of the family on west with him and make a new start for all of us."

"You make him sound like a devoted family man," said Longarm.

"He was! He loved his family! That's why he did what he did, to provide for them. You see, he'd been a failure at everything else he'd ever tried. He lost his farm, and he had a store that went under, and nothing seemed to work for him. So he decided to do something really audacious, so that if he failed again, at least it would be a spectacular failure."

"But instead, the only thing he was successful at was being a murderer and a thief."

"He didn't like it," argued Melinda. "But he had a wife and a lot of children and grandchildren back in Ohio, and he was determined to make himself a rich man so he could take care of them."

"You still haven't told me how you know about all of this," Longarm pointed out.

"When Grandfather went back to Ohio, he found that his wife—my grandmother—had passed away while he was gone. There was a cholera epidemic. A lot of people died. My grandmother, and most of the rest of my family. But my mother was alive, and me and my older brother. Grandpa moved in with us. He was a bitter man. He had sacrificed so much, and most of the people he'd done it for were dead."

Longarm frowned. "Are you telling me that your grandfather spun this whole yarn of bloodshed and thievery to his *grandkids*?"

Melinda shook her head. "No. He told my brother— David—and me that he had a treasure map hidden inside his hat and that one day we'd all be rich when he went and dug it up. I don't think we really believed him, though. Well, maybe I did, a little. David said that Grandpa was just telling stories, like fairy tales. Then, after he'd lived with us for a couple of years on our farm, there was an accident. Grandpa was replacing an axle on our wagon. The wagon slipped off the blocks and fell on him. It crushed him . . . killed him. That was the end of his dream."

And a better end than William O'Sullivan had probably deserved, the bloody-handed old pirate, thought Longarm. He didn't say that, though.

"A few years after that," Melinda went on, "David and I found an envelope full of papers that Grandpa had written and stuffed into an old Bible. It was sealed up and addressed to the two of us, and it said we should open it if anything ever happened to him. The whole story was inside, so we would know that he'd been telling the truth and that there really were several chests full of treasure buried in Abaddon. He wanted us to go after them and get them for ourselves. That was his legacy to his grandchildren."

"A mighty bloody legacy," said Longarm.

"I thought so, too. I didn't want any of the money. I thought that if David and I ever found it, we ought to try to give it back to whoever it rightfully belonged to. But I was a twelve-year-old girl. I didn't know much about the world yet."

"So your brother talked you out of it."

She shook her head. "He didn't get a chance to. He was killed less than a year later when a runaway team of horses trampled him. That left just me and my mother to survive on our own, whatever it took." Her voice caught a little as she added, "And it took . . . a lot."

Longarm didn't say anything for a moment. Then, "I'm sorry. I reckon it was mighty hard on you and your ma, both."

"Hard enough that eventually it killed her, too. But I did what I had to do to get enough money to come to Texas and hire those men and wagons. I'm going to dig up those chests, Custis. Nothing is going to stop me."

"And I reckon you don't plan to give the loot back anymore."

"My grandfather wanted me to have it. I'm the only one of the family left. It belongs to me as much as it does to anybody, and I intend to do what Grandpa wanted."

"That's a mighty touching story, but when it comes right down to it, that's blood money, Melinda. It won't ever make you happy."

Melinda laughed. "Now *you're* the one spinning fairy tales, Custis. That money is going to make me very happy indeed."

If she really felt that way—and she sounded sincere— then he wasn't going to be able to talk her out of it. Which meant that he had to stop her somehow from carrying out her plan. The sort of piracy that O'Sullivan and his gang had carried out didn't really fall under Longarm's jurisdiction as a federal lawman, but it definitely crossed the line where his sense of justice was concerned. Maybe some of the relatives of the pilgrims O'Sullivan had robbed and murdered could be found. If that was the case, the loot ought to be returned to them. If not, well, there were charities that could put it to good use.

On the other hand, it wasn't like he had never bent the law to serve a higher purpose in the past. And from the sound of it, Melinda had led a difficult life. Did that entitle her to the loot that her grandfather had buried out there, north of the well?

Longarm couldn't answer that question.

Melinda went on. "The problem now, Custis, is what are we going to do with you? I don't suppose you'd promise to go on about your business and never tell anyone about what I've just told you, would you?"

Damn it, he wished she hadn't put it quite so bluntly. That was the ethical dilemma he'd just been wrestling with.

He didn't have to answer, though, because at that moment someone tapped him on the foot. He glanced down and saw Haygood McCready crouched underneath the wagon. The deputy sheriff must have crawled under there from his place under the next wagon. There was no telling how much of Melinda's story he had overheard.

McCready pointed to himself, then jabbed a thumb upward toward the wagon to indicate that he would deal with Melinda. He started crawling backward like a doodlebug.

"Damn it, Custis," said Melinda, "am I going to have to kill you?"

Well, that changed things a mite. If she was willing to kill a deputy U.S. marshal to get her hands on that loot, then Longarm figured she didn't deserve to have it. So he stalled by asking her, "Do Barstow and his men know what you're after?"

"No, you're the only one. I'm sure they've figured out that there's something valuable here, but they don't know what it is."

Longarm couldn't see McCready at all anymore. He said, "How do you know they won't double-cross you and try to take the loot for themselves once it's dug up?"

From the frown that appeared suddenly on her face, he could tell that maybe she hadn't considered that possibility. She blustered, "I won't let them."

"How's one woman going to stop six men from doing whatever they want to do?"

She looked at him for a long moment, then said, "You could stop them."

Longarm's eyebrows rose in surprise. "Me?"

"That's right. Half the money, Custis . . . and me." She smiled at him. "It's a good bargain. You'd be a lot richer man than you ever will be working for the government."

"And you'd rather have half the money than none."

"There's enough for two," she said. "We could both be happy that way."

Longarm sighed. "One of us would be, anyway."

"Oh, you'd be happy. I'd make sure of that."

"Sorry. I'm right fond of being able to sleep at night."

"You won't even consider it?"

"Nothing to consider," said Longarm. Looking through the wagon, he saw Haygood McCready's tall black hat rising through the opening at the front.

Suddenly, the wagon rocked on its thoroughbraces as McCready vaulted into it with an agility belying his age. Melinda gave a startled cry and tried to twist around and bring her gun to bear on the deputy sheriff, but Longarm was already moving. He dropped the hat and the map and lunged over the tailgate, reaching for Melinda's gun arm.

He closed his hand around her wrist and jerked upward just as she pulled the trigger. The pistol blasted, but the bullet tore harmlessly through the canvas cover over the wagon bed.

A quick twist of her wrist made Melinda cry out in pain and drop the gun. Longarm caught it with his other hand and let go of her, stepping back. McCready said, "Much obliged for not lettin' that gal shoot me, Marshal. I figured that me jumpin' into the wagon'd distract her enough you could grab that little ol' popgun."

Even though the pistol was small-caliber, the shot had been loud enough to be heard all over Abaddon. As Longarm backed away from the wagon, he saw Barstow and the other men hurrying toward him with guns drawn and worried looks on their faces.

"Hold it," he called to them. "Everything's all right—"

He didn't get to finish, because at that moment, Melinda tore her shirt open to reveal her bare breasts. She leaned out the back of the wagon and screamed, "Oh, my God, he tried to rape me! *Get him!*"

Chapter 10

Barstow and the other men came to an abrupt halt and stood there for a second, staring. The unexpected sight of a beautiful, bare-breasted woman would do that to most hombres, thought Longarm, nailing them right there in their tracks.

That moment of hesitation gave Longarm the chance he needed. He whirled toward Barstow and the other men, his right hand flashing across his body to the Colt in the cross-draw rig. He already had Melinda's gun in his left hand, and less than a heartbeat later, he had the Colt out, too. He leveled both irons at the men and said again, louder this time, "Hold it!"

They had their guns drawn, but the weapons were pointed toward the ground, rather than being raised. Barstow glared at Longarm and asked angrily, "What the hell's going on here?"

"Just take it easy, old son," Longarm advised him. "Whatever you're thinking, it's likely wrong."

"Yeah," added McCready from the wagon. "Why, we never laid nary a hand on this here girl—"

"They're lying!" Melinda insisted. "They tried to rape me." She clutched her torn shirt over her breasts now, looking pitiful as she even managed to sniffle a little. "They . . . they started ripping my clothes off—"

"That's a dang-blasted lie!" exclaimed McCready.

Barstow said, "Why don't you put those guns down, Marshal, and we'll get to the bottom of this?"

"We've already told you the truth," said Longarm. "We didn't attack Miss Kelly."

"She says you did. And you may have the drop on us, but even with two guns, I don't reckon you can down all of us before we manage to get some lead into you."

"I reckon you'd better think twice about threatening a federal lawman like that."

Barstow was right, though. There were five of them, and their revolvers were already in their hands, so it was unlikely that—

Longarm's thoughts came to an abrupt halt as he realized that he was facing only five men, Barstow and four others. But counting the outriders, there had been *six* men with the wagons.

He had started to jerk his head around to look for the sixth man when the hard pounding of hoofbeats suddenly came from somewhere close behind him. He twisted and tried to throw himself aside, but it was too late. The sixth man, mounted on one of the saddle horses, galloped at him, yelling at the horse. Longarm managed to avoid being trampled, but he couldn't get completely out of the way. The horse's shoulder struck him with stunning force as it rushed past. He felt himself sailing through the air from the impact of the collision.

"Get him!" shouted Barstow.

Longarm hit the ground, and even though it was sandy,

he landed hard enough that Melinda's pistol was jolted out of his grip. He hung on to his Colt, but only for a second. Then one of the men kicked his wrist and sent the gun flying out of his hand as they crowded around him.

Longarm grabbed a man's leg and heaved hard, upending the hombre. As the man went down with a startled yell, he tangled with the legs of another man and brought him down, too. That gave Longarm enough of an opening to roll over a couple of times and surge to his feet.

He saw Barstow and two more of the men closing in on him. They had holstered their guns, now that he was unarmed, but they had their fists clenched, and judging by the expressions on their faces, they intended to give him a hell of a beating.

McCready had pushed past Melinda in the wagon, though, and thrust his long-barreled Remington at them. "You fellers hold it right there!" the deputy sheriff ordered. "I'll ventilate the first hombre that moves—"

"Watch out, Haygood!" Longarm called, but the warning came too late. Melinda loomed up behind McCready and swung some sort of small keg at his head. The keg shattered as it crashed into McCready's head and shoulders, sending an explosion of sugar or flour or whatever it was into the air, and at the same time knocking McCready headfirst out of the wagon. He landed in a crumpled, senseless heap.

That left Barstow and the others free to rush Longarm again. They came in with fists flying, and all he could do was try to block as many of the punches as he could and deal out some punishment of his own. He felt and heard the too-small shirt ripping across the shoulders and down the arms as he lashed out with his fists. His knuckles slammed into Barstow's jaw and knocked the wagon master back-

ward. A second later, as a blow grazed his ear, Longarm
twisted and hooked a hard left into the belly of another
man. The hombre bent over in breathless pain. Longarm
raised a knee into his jaw and sent him sprawling.

A third man grabbed him from behind, and he saw
then that the man who had nearly ridden him down had
dismounted and joined the fight, too. That man came in
and smashed brutal punches into Longarm's midsection
as the man behind held the big lawman's arms. Longarm
grunted as he absorbed the punishment. His legs were still
free, so he lifted a booted foot into the groin of the man
who was punching him. The varmint let out a high-
pitched scream and staggered back, clutching at himself
before he fell down and began curling up in a ball around
the agony that radiated out from his balls.

Barstow was back in the fight, though, and he whipped
a punch that landed on Longarm's jaw and made fire-
works explode behind his eyes. Longarm knew another
blow like that would knock him out. He went limp in the
arms of the man holding him. His weight dragged both of
them toward the ground. Longarm drove an elbow back
into the man's belly and tore loose from his grip.

Diving forward, Longarm rammed into Barstow's legs
and knocked them out from under the wagon master. All
three men sprawled in a tangled pile on the ground. Longarm scrambled free. He pushed himself to his feet again
but froze as Melinda said, "I'll shoot you, Custis, I swear
I will."

He looked at her and saw that she had climbed out of
the wagon and retrieved the Remington that McCready
had dropped. It took both hands for her to hold the heavy
revolver steady, which meant she couldn't hold her torn
shirt together anymore. It hung all the way open, and her

bare breasts heaved from the emotion that gripped her as she glared at Longarm over the barrel of the gun. For a fairly petite young woman, at that moment she looked like a damn Amazon, he thought.

And since she had the Remington cocked and ready to blow a hole in him, he sighed and lifted his hands. "All right, take it easy, Melinda," he told her. "Nobody needs to die here."

"I'm not so sure about that," she said. "I think it would be easier if you and Deputy McCready were both dead."

Barstow was clambering to his feet as Melinda said that. He gaped at her and said, "Hold on there, ma'am. You're talking about murdering a couple of lawmen. We didn't sign on for that, even if they did try to attack you."

"Then what *did* you sign on for, Mr. Barstow?" she snapped at him. "You had to know that there was some-thing a little shady about this deal, otherwise I wouldn't have sworn you to secrecy and made it worth your while to go along with that."

Barstow shrugged. "I might've had a suspicion or two, but I still say they didn't include killing a pair of badge toters, especially when one of 'em is a federal man."

Even as he was talking, he had a hard time keeping his eyes off Melinda's breasts. The other men were getting an eyeful, too, except for the one Longarm had kicked in the balls. He was still hurting too much to be concerned about anything else.

"All right," Melinda said. "I don't particularly want to kill anybody, either, unless there's no other choice. Take them into the trading post and tie them up. Make sure they can't get loose. We'll leave them here when we go."

"That's the same thing as murder," said Longarm. "If we can't get loose, we're liable to die of thirst."

Melinda shook her head. "I'll leave an anonymous note for the marshal in Brimstone. He can come out here and turn you loose. You'll get thirsty, but you won't die. By the time you get back to town, though, I'll be long gone."

"What about us?" asked Barstow. "These wagons can't travel all that fast, Miss Kelly. I reckon Long would have a chance to come after us."

Melinda frowned. "That's true. And now that I think about it, I'll need the wagons . . ." She shook her head. "I'll figure it out later. For now, put them in the trading post and tie them up, like I said. And then . . . we'll have some digging to do."

Longarm knew she meant digging up those chests full of loot her grandfather had buried all those years ago. But he also knew that once she figured out how much easier it would be on her if he and McCready were dead, there was a good chance some grave digging might be involved, too.

Barstow and one of the outriders took Longarm into the trading post at gunpoint, while the other two drivers carried in McCready's still unconscious form. Longarm had to sit down on the sand-covered floor with his back against the counter while Barstow tied him hand and foot with rope from one of the wagons. McCready was trussed up, as well, and left lying on the floor near Longarm.

"Sorry about this, Marshal," Barstow said as he straightened from the chore.

"You know Miss Kelly's lying about what happened out there, don't you?" asked Longarm.

A wry grin split Barstow's face. "I reckon that's probably true. But that little lady's up to something that involves a lot of money, or I'll eat my hat. I figure there's bound to be a way for my pards and me to wind up with our share of that payoff." He chuckled. "Maybe even more than our share."

That comment didn't surprise Longarm. Melinda had been a fool to put her trust in these men. Maybe they weren't actually outlaws, but many a man would turn crooked if presented with the opportunity. Longarm saw the light of greed shining in Barstow's eyes, and nothing but that buried loot would put it out.

Barstow and the others clomped out of the trading post, leaving Longarm and McCready there. Longarm tested the bonds around his wrists and could tell that Barstow had done a good job on them. There was a slight chance he could work his way loose, but it would take hours, at the very least, and would cost him a lot of skin.

McCready groaned and started to stir. Consciousness was trying to seep back into his brain. Longarm's legs were stretched out in front of him. Even though his ankles were tied tightly together, he was able to move his legs over until he could nudge McCready's shoulder with his feet.

"Wake up, Haygood."

"Huh?" muttered McCready. "Wh . . . wha . . . what in blazes . . ." His eyelids fluttered open. He tried to move his arms and legs and wound up just flopping around a little. "Well, I'll be a son of a lop-eared mule!" he exclaimed. "Marshal, is that you?"

"It's me," said Longarm.

"What the hell happened to us?"

"What do you *think* happened to us?"

McCready groaned again. "That gal," he said bitterly. "Last thing I recollect, she was a-bellerin' and a-carryin' on about how you tried to mo-lest her, and Barstow and them other fellers believed what she was sayin' and jumped on you, and I tried to get 'em to stop, and . . .

and I don't rightly know what happened after that."

"That's because the gal busted a keg of flour or sugar over your head and knocked you out."

McCready licked his lips. "Yeah, this ol' skull o' mine does feel like somebody fetched it a right smart wallop."

"I was a little worried at first that she'd killed you."

McCready shook his head, then winced in pain at the movement. "It'd take more'n that to put me under the ground permanent-like. They tied us up, did they?"

"Yeah. Barstow and his friends were ready to do just about anything for her once they got a good look at her bare bosom. They figured out there might be some money involved, too."

"Dadgummit. I mostly missed the bare bosom part. I heard the gal tellin' you all about how her granddaddy was really a owlhoot, though. That was quite a yarn she was spinnin'. You reckon it's true?"

"I'm convinced she believes it is. The only way to be sure what O'Sullivan buried out there, though, is to dig it up. I expect that's what they've gone to do now."

McCready wriggled and twisted around until he was next to the counter, then got a shoulder against it and gradually worked his way into a sitting position.

"We best get back to back and see if'n we can untie each other," he suggested. "Once Barstow and them other fellers feast their eyes on all that loot, it won't take 'em long to figure out it'll be better for them if the two of us are dead."

"That's true, but they did a pretty good job of tying us up. I'm not sure we can get loose."

"Well, hell, it's worth a try, ain't it? Better'n sittin' down and dyin', like you told me durin' that sandstorm."

"Yeah, it's better than that," said Longarm. He turned

away from McCready, who did likewise. They scooted toward each other until they could reach the ropes.

As they worked on the knots, Longarm could hear the voices of the men outside, calling to each other, although he couldn't make out the words. They were probably trying to follow that old treasure map of O'Sullivan's, he thought. With each minute that went by, he and McCready might be that much closer to death, because Barstow and the others were that much closer to finding the chests and discovering what was at stake here.

"You . . . uh . . . makin' any progress, Marshal?" asked McCready over his shoulder.

"Don't seem to be," replied Longarm. "How about you?"

"Nary a bit. That son of a bitch knows how to tie a good, tight knot."

The wind was getting up a little, Longarm realized. It was louder now as it blew through the trading post, and its currents stirred the sand on the floor. Longarm might have been mistaken, but he thought the light outside wasn't as bright, either, indicating that a sandy haze was blocking some of the sun's rays.

He paused in his futile efforts to untie McCready and said, "Does it sound to you like another storm might be blowing up?"

McCready stopped fumbling at the knots on Longarm's wrists and listened to the wind. "Maybe," he said after a moment. "Hard to tell. The wind blows a lot out here anyway."

"I thought you didn't know that much about this desert."

"Well, I'm just talkin' about deserts in general. Hell, there's always some sort o' big ol' sandstorm a-blowin' up in 'em, ain't there?"

"Yeah, I reckon. If it gets too bad, though, Melinda and Barstow and the others won't be able to start back to Brimstone right away. They'll have to wait for it to blow over."

"Ain't sure that'll help us none. They can go ahead and kill us whether they leave right away or not."

McCready had a point there. After what Longarm and Melinda had shared the night before—on top of this very counter, in fact—Longarm didn't want to think that she would stand by and allow him to be murdered . . . but he knew that the prospect of wealth changed some people, made them do things they never would have done otherwise.

He was about to get back to struggling with the knots of McCready's bonds when he heard heavy footsteps clomping on the porch outside. Barstow appeared in the open doorway, a big grin on his face. That grin made Longarm's heart sink.

So did the fact that Barstow drew a knife from a sheath on his belt as he started across the room toward them. "Trying to get loose, are you?" he asked. "Well, I can't say as I blame you. But I'm too good with a rope. You fellas could've worked at that for a couple of days and not gotten anywhere."

He reached down with the knife and cut the bonds around Longarm's ankles. Stepping back quickly, just in case Longarm tried to kick him, he moved over and did the same with the ropes on McCready's ankles. Then he moved well out of reach, sheathed the knife, and pulled his gun.

"Your legs are free now. Get up. You're goin' for a little walk."

"Getting up is easier said than done with your hands tied behind your back," Longarm pointed out.

Barstow shrugged. "I can shoot you right there and drag you out."

"Keep your goldurn britches on," said McCready as he started trying to struggle to his feet. "We're gettin' up. Come on, Marshal."

Longarm braced his back against the counter and started working his way up. It took a couple of minutes, but he and McCready made it to their feet. Longarm was unsteady because his legs had gone numb. Feeling began to return to them with a sensation like a million tiny knives jabbing into his flesh.

McCready seemed to be suffering from the same affliction. He swayed and had to lean against the counter for support.

Barstow gestured with the gun. "Let's go. Outside, both of you."

After a moment, Longarm and McCready were able to walk. They headed toward the door. Barstow moved aside so he could cover them as they went out. He followed them and ordered, "Down by the well."

As they walked toward the eastern end of the building, Longarm asked, "Did it turn out to be fifty feet or fifty yards from the well?"

"Fifty paces," said Barstow. "It took us a little while to work that out."

"How many chests are there?"

"Three. And they're nice and full, too. I never saw so many greenbacks and so much jewelry in one place before."

Longarm bit back a curse. He had been clinging to a slender hope that O'Sullivan's so-called "treasure" would turn out to be worthless, or at least something that wasn't worth killing over, but obviously, that wasn't the case. The old pirate hadn't been lying to his grandchildren. He really had buried a fortune in the sands at Abaddon.

A surprise waited for him when he rounded the corner of the building, but not too much of one. He saw the heaps of sand that had been dug out and the three large wooden chests sitting on the ground next to the big hole. The other five men were nearby, guns drawn.

Melinda Kelly stood next to the hole, too, but she wasn't in charge anymore. In fact, her hands were tied behind her back, too, just like Longarm's and McCready's. That was the little surprise. As the rising wind blew her long dark hair around her face, she turned her head and looked at Longarm. Her face was pale, and he saw the fear in her eyes. Barstow and the other men had double-crossed her, just as Longarm had warned her might happen.

He hadn't expected them to kill Melinda, though, at least not yet. He supposed the loot meant more to them than a beautiful young woman. With enough money, a man could have a never-ending supply of beautiful young women.

"Custis . . ." she began.

Longarm shook his head. It was too late for talk now.

He was curious about one thing, though. He turned to look at Barstow and asked, "You fellas ain't going back to Brimstone, are you?"

"Nope," Barstow said. "We've got plenty of water and supplies. We're going on west. We'll be in El Paso in a few days, and from there we can live high on the hog in Mexico for the rest of our lives."

"And all you have to do is kill the three of us."

"Yep. That's right." Barstow raised his gun and leveled it at Longarm's head. "You and the old-timer move on up to the edge of the hole, Long. We went to all the trouble of digging it, so we might as well get some more use out of it."

Chapter 11

"Please," Melinda begged. "You don't have to kill us. Just take the money and go. We won't even tell anyone about it. Will we, Custis?"

Barstow laughed and shook his head before Longarm even had a chance to answer. "Don't waste your breath, ma'am. I know the sort of hombre this lawman is. He'd get on our trail, and he'd never rest until he caught up with us and evened the score. Isn't that right, Marshal?"

"I reckon that's about what would happen, all right," said Longarm. There was no point in lying. Barstow had made up his mind.

"No, the only thing for it is to kill the three of you and let the desert have you. You'll be as lost as Abaddon was before that storm blew through and uncovered it."

"Acts like another storm is coming up, Barstow," Longarm said. "I ain't sure you'll make it very far if you set out now."

"Well, we can afford to wait. Like I said, we have plenty of water and supplies."

"So you don't need to kill us right now."

Barstow shook his head. "No point in putting it off."

Melinda began to cry.

"You ornery, no-good polecats!" yelled McCready. "Gonna shoot us down like dogs, are you?"

"That's the idea." Barstow pointed his gun at the deputy sheriff's head. "You want to go first, old man?"

For a second, Longarm thought Barstow had fired without waiting for an answer, because a shot roared even as the words came out of Barstow's mouth. But then more guns blasted and one of Barstow's men let out a gurgling scream as a slug tore away half of his jaw.

Longarm wasn't sure what was going on, but as far as he could tell, somebody had opened fire on Barstow and the others. They were bound to put up a fight against the bushwhackers, though, which meant that a hell of a lot of lead was about to be flying around in the air.

Longarm lunged toward Melinda and bulled into her. She let out a startled cry as the collision knocked both of them off their feet and sent them plummeting into the hole where O'Sullivan's loot had been buried.

At least down there they would be out of the direct line of fire, thought Longarm as he slammed painfully into the ground at the bottom of the hole.

A second later, Haygood McCready came flying into the hole as well, yelling as he fell. Longarm didn't think McCready had been hit, but it was hard to tell for sure. He figured the deputy sheriff had had the same idea about getting out of the way of all those bullets buzzing around.

"You all right, Haygood?" Longarm asked.

"Yeah," McCready answered. "Think I shook about half my teeth out landin' so hard, though . . . and I ain't got all that many left that I can spare!"

"How about you, Melinda?"

"I . . . I'm not shot," she said. "But what happened up there, Custis? I . . . I thought Mr. Barstow and the others were about to kill us. Did they start shooting at each other instead?"

That was too far-fetched a notion for Longarm to believe. Lurking in the back of his head was an idea about what had happened. If he was right, he and McCready and Melinda might not be any better off in the long run, but at least they were still alive right now.

"Melinda, roll over so that you're facing away from me."

"What?"

"Just do what I said." If they had any chance, even the slimmest one, Longarm intended to seize it for all it was worth. Barstow might not have taken the same amount of time and trouble tying up Melinda, since he wouldn't have considered her as much of a threat as the two lawmen.

Melinda rolled onto her side. Longarm put his back to her and felt for the bonds around her wrists. Sure enough, they had a little more play in them, he found, as he tugged at the strands of rope.

Above them, the battle continued. Gunshots blasted out from all around. Men cursed and yelled in pain. A horse's hoofbeats clattered off into the distance. The wind was blowing even stronger now. Longarm gritted his teeth as he worked at Melinda's bonds. He wished he could see what was going on.

Suddenly, the ropes were loose around Melinda's wrists. "Pull out of them!" he told her. "As soon as you're free, see if you can untie me!"

A moment later, he felt Melinda's slender fingers moving against his wrists as she struggled to untie the knots. "They're . . . too tight!" she gasped. "I can't get them!"

"Keep trying," Longarm urged her. If he had his arms free, he might be able to get his hands on a gun. That could change things in a hurry.

"I'm sorry, Custis, it's just too hard . . . Wait a minute! I think I've got one of them starting to come loose!"

Longarm twisted his wrists carefully. He didn't want to tighten the knots again if Melinda had actually loosened them. He felt a little play in the rope that hadn't been there before.

"That's right," he said. "A little more now."

The shots seemed to be dying away. That wasn't really a good sign. He and McCready didn't have any friends out here that he knew of, so whichever side emerged victorious, it probably wouldn't be good for them.

He tilted his head back and looked up. The sky was the same yellowish-gray that it had been a couple of days earlier, obscuring the sun and casting a pall over the landscape. There was another storm blowing in, and while it might not be as strong as the one that had uncovered Abaddon, it was an added problem right now, when Longarm didn't need one.

He pushed that thought out of his mind and concentrated on Melinda's efforts to untie him. "That's it," he said softly as he felt her working on the knots. "Keep going."

Suddenly, she jerked on one strand of rope and pulled it completely off his wrists. "I've got it!" she cried. "I've got it!"

Longarm twisted his wrists again, felt the rope sliding over his skin. The muscles in his arms and shoulders bunched and knotted in the torn shirt as he wrenched at the bonds. The ropes scraped painfully at his skin, but he didn't care. Any blood would just make them slicker.

With a grunt, he tore free from the ropes. His hands were numb and clumsy as he brought them around in front of him. Some of the bonds still dangled from them. Crimson ran from the abrasions on his wrists. But he was free, and that was what mattered, he thought, as he flexed his fingers to hurry some feeling back into them.

The hole where the chests had been buried was about ten feet deep, but the sides sloped down instead of being sheer. Longarm began trying to scramble to the surface, but it wasn't easy in the loose sand.

"Hey, what about me?" McCready called behind him.

"I'll be back for you, Haygood," Longarm replied. "Right now I've got to see if I can find a gun!"

Using his hands and feet almost like he was swimming, he climbed up the side of the pit. Shots still roared, but now the reports sounded like they were coming from somewhere among the buildings of Abaddon.

Longarm reached the top and felt the sting of windborne particles of sand against his face. He looked around, and saw one of Barstow's men sprawled facedown nearby. The man's revolver still lay near his empty hand, where he had dropped it. Longarm hurried toward the gun.

A shot blasted before he could reach the weapon. The bullet plowed into the ground just in front of Longarm and kicked up a lot of dust, which was swirled away by the wind. Longarm stopped short, knowing that if he tried to reach the Colt, he would be gunned down.

"Don't move!" a harsh voice ordered, confirming that hunch. "I'd be plumb happy to kill you, you damned lawdog!"

Longarm turned his head and saw Colonel Garth standing on the other side of the hole in the sand. The burly outlaw's gun was leveled at Longarm, and Garth's lips were pulled back from his teeth in a savage, murderous snarl.

The first thing Longarm had thought of when somebody opened fire on Barstow and the other men was that Garth's bunch must have found them at last. So he wasn't particularly surprised to see the bank robber and killer.

What happened next shocked him to his core, though. From inside the pit, Haygood McCready called, "Damn it, Colonel, it took you long enough! Now get me outta this here hole in the ground!"

"Keep your shirt on, Uncle Haygood," said Garth. "First I've gotta decide whether to go ahead and kill this blasted lawman."

His eyes wide with surprise, Longarm looked into the hole and saw McCready looking up at him. "Sorry, Marshal," the old-timer said. "Reckon what I been tellin' you all along ain't quite the truth."

Longarm grunted. He said, "Reckon not," in a flat voice. Then he looked across the pit at the outlaw on the other side and went on. "Take it easy, Garth. There's no need for anybody else to die here."

Garth's lip curled even more. "That's what you say. You killed three of my friends, lawman. Worse than that, you played me for a fool."

"Damn it, Colonel," said McCready. "You can cuss the marshal later. Get me outta here."

"All right, all right, hold your horses." Keeping the gun leveled at Longarm, Garth pulled a knife from its sheath at his waist and tossed it down into the hole. He ordered Melinda, "Take that knife and cut my uncle loose, girl."

She called up to Longarm. "Custis . . . ?"

"Damn it, do what I told you!" roared Garth.

"Go ahead," Longarm told her. They had no choice but to play along with the outlaws . . . for now.

Melinda picked up the knife and quickly but carefully sawed through the ropes around McCready's wrists. Then McCready took the blade from her and climbed out of the pit.

"Where's the rest of your bunch?" he asked Garth.

"At the trading post. They've got the three men who're left alive holed up in that blacksmith shop, the same place where we stayed last night. I left them there and came to get you." Garth nodded toward Longarm. "And to deal with this bastard."

"Take it easy," said McCready, echoing Longarm's words from a few moments earlier. "There ain't no need to start rushin' things. I know you got a grudge against the marshal here, but we been together for a couple o' days, and he ain't a bad sort. Saved my life, he did."

"And killed three of my men! Plus he's a lawman. You know good and well the only good badge toter is a dead badge toter, Uncle Haygood."

McCready nodded slowly. "That is true as the Gospel," he said.

An occasional shot came from the old settlement as Iron Mike Dumont and Hair-Trigger Thompson swapped lead with whoever was holed up in the blacksmith shop. Longarm didn't know if Barstow had survived the ambush, and he didn't really care. He was trying to figure a way out of the dangerous predicament in which he and Melinda found themselves. He was reminded of the old saying about jumping from the frying pan into the fire.

At the moment, the thing to do seemed to be to keep McCready talking. Longarm said, "I reckon it's safe to assume you ain't really a deputy sheriff from Crockett County, Haygood."

"Nor from any other county, neither," agreed McCready. "I'm afraid I took that old tin star off a feller who was tryin' to arrest me a long time ago. Been carryin' it around ever since. Comes in handy ever' now and then, like when I showed it to you."

"What were you supposed to do, meet your nephew and the rest of his gang here in the desert?"

"That's right. I been through this here desert before and had a pretty good idea where this ol' ghost town was. Didn't have no idea at the time that the sand had completely covered it up. I figured to meet Colonel and his boys, then we'd find that ol' well and dig it out, and then I'd guide 'em on to the other side o' the desert. I'm sorta retired from the owlhoot business, you understand, but hell, blood's blood. I couldn't say no to my sister's boy when he wrote to me and told me what he was plannin'."

"But then that sandstorm came along, spooked your mule, and left you afoot."

"Yep. Pure-dee bad luck, all the way around. Reckon I would've died if you hadn't come along, Marshal."

"So after we found Abaddon, you started all that signaling in hopes that Garth and the others would see it if they survived the storm like we did."

McCready nodded. "That's right. It worked, too. They come in last night. I slipped 'em into town and hid 'em at the smithy." The old-timer turned his head to glare at Garth. "How come you and your pards just sat in there and didn't do nothin' earlier when those varmints jumped us in the street?"

"Hell, we didn't know what was goin' on," replied Garth with a defensive air. "And we couldn't very well start blazin' away with you right in the middle of them, Uncle Haygood."

"You done that exact same thing later," McCready pointed out.

Garth shrugged. "By then we figured there wasn't any choice. That bastard was about to shoot you anyway."

"Yeah, he was," McCready admitted. "Anyway, you come through in time to save us. You done good, Colonel."

Garth grinned. "Now, what's this all about? What's in those chests?" He nodded toward the chests, which still sat on the sand near the hole where they had been buried.

"Take a gander for your ownself," McCready advised.

From the pit, Melinda called, "Is anybody going to help me out of here?"

"Keep your shirt on, gal." McCready chuckled. "Which, from what I hear, is somethin' you have a mite of a hard time doin'."

Longarm glanced into the hole and saw that Melinda looked angry and embarrassed at the same time. She had pulled her shirt together in front and tied it closed as best she could, but there were still several gaps with an impressive amount of rounded female flesh showing through.

Garth handed his gun to McCready and said, "Keep that star-packin' son of a bitch covered." Then he went over to the nearest chest, unfastened the catch, and lifted the lid.

An awed whistle came from the outlaw as he gazed into the chest and saw stacks and stacks of greenbacks, along with a welter of rings, bracelets, necklaces, and other jewelry. Longarm could see the loot from where he was, and he had to admit, it was an impressive display. If the other two chests were equally full, it would all add up to a fortune, no doubt about that.

"Shit fire, Uncle Haygood!" said Garth. "We're rich!"

"That we are, boy," McCready agreed.

"Did you know about this?"

"Not until a little while ago. I heard the gal tellin' the marshal all about it. Seems her grandpa was the one who founded this town, but it was really just a trick to lure wagon trains through the desert so him and his gang could ambush 'em and loot 'em. That's the take from the scheme."

"I reckon our luck's turned. We made it through that storm, and now we're fuckin' rich. All we got to do is kill the marshal and those other three assholes."

McCready frowned. "Watch your language, boy. Don't you know there's a female present?"

"Damn right I know. We're takin' her with us, ain't we?"

McCready glanced at the sky. "I don't reckon we're goin' anywheres right now. Not with another bad storm comin' in. We're gonna have to hole up here in the settlement until it blows over."

"Well, then, the gal will help us pass the time, won't she?"

Down in the pit, Melinda swallowed hard. She had to be imagining what was going to happen to her at the hands of Garth and the other outlaws, thought Longarm. He glanced at McCready. The old-timer didn't look happy about it, but Longarm didn't figure McCready would try to stop Garth and the others from doing anything they wanted to do.

"First things first," said Garth. He slammed the lid of the chest, then came back over and reclaimed his gun from McCready. "We got to kill those three hombres in the blacksmith shop."

"What about the marshal?" asked McCready.

Garth shrugged. "I reckon we can let him live awhile longer. Now that I think about it, makin' sure that he dies long and slow and hard will help pass the time while we're waitin' for that sandstorm to blow over, too."

That wasn't a very appealing prospect, thought Longarm, but it beat the hell out of being gunned down right now and dumped back into that hole. As long as he was alive, there was always a chance he could turn the tables on his captors.

Garth used the revolver in his hand to gesture at the pit. "Help the girl out, Long."

Longarm nodded. He lay down at the edge of the hole and extended a hand as far as he could reach toward Melinda. "Grab hold," he told her. "I'll help you climb out of there."

She had to climb a short distance up the side before she could grasp Longarm's hand, and that took her several tries as she kept sliding back down in the loose sand. But finally she managed to clasp her fingers around his wrist, and he caught hold of hers as well. With his help, she was able to clamber up out of the pit without too much trouble. Then he stood up and helped her to her feet.

Her face was close to his as she whispered, "I'm so sorry, Custis. I . . . I wish I had never gotten you into this mess."

"It ain't all your fault," he said. "Although I ain't forgotten that you were ready to kill me a time or two."

She shook her head. "I wouldn't have. Not really. I could never do that."

Garth snapped, "Whatever you two are palaverin'

about over there, break it up! Come on around that hole. We're goin' back to town."

With Garth and McCready behind them, Longarm and Melinda walked the short distance back to Abaddon. Longarm glanced at the sky. The sun had disappeared completely again, and the air was thick with blowing sand. He hadn't heard any shots for a while, but the wind was loud now and might have carried the sounds away.

When they reached the eastern end of the trading post, where the well was located, Longarm saw that the sand was already starting to drift a little against the wall of sandstone blocks. If that drift grew high enough, it would spill over the wall and start to fill the well again. The storm that had come through a couple of days earlier had been extraordinarily fierce, he knew, otherwise it wouldn't have uncovered the buildings of the lost settlement as it had. But it had only lasted ten or twelve hours. Sometimes these big blows could go on for several days, or even a week. If that happened now, the well might be full of sand again by the time the winds finally died down.

But he wouldn't be alive by then unless he figured out some way to whittle down the odds against him, he reminded himself, so he really couldn't worry about the well now.

"We're goin' in the back," said Garth. "If we go out on the street, those bastards in the blacksmith shop are liable to take some potshots at us."

"You say there's three of 'em left?" asked McCready.

"Yeah, and some of them may be wounded, for all we know. We killed one out by that hole in the ground, and then downed two more when they made a run for the town. The fightin' was pretty hot and heavy for a little while. But then the three that were left went to ground inside the blacksmith shop."

"Only one way outta there, right?"

Garth nodded. "Yeah. That's why we've been able to keep 'em pinned down, because we can cover the door from inside the tradin' post. The walls of that old shop are thick, though."

"They're thick," said McCready as he rubbed at his stubbled chin and frowned in thought, "but I reckon they'll burn."

A grin spread across Garth's bearded face. "Damn right they will, if we can figure out a way to set 'em on fire."

"You got any whiskey left in your saddlebags?"

Garth shook his head. "Nope. But I'll bet there might be some in those wagons. Maybe some coal oil for lanterns, too."

"We'll have a look in a little while. Right now, let's go inside, and you can introduce me to your pards."

Garth nodded toward Longarm and Melinda. "What about these two?"

"Well, I sort of hate to say it," replied McCready with a chuckle, "but I reckon we're gonna have to tie 'em up again."

Chapter 12

They went through the trading post's rear door and found Dumont and Thompson in the main room, crouched next to the front windows. From time to time, one of the outlaws snapped a shot at the door of the blacksmith shop across the street, whenever one of the men inside risked poking his head out long enough to throw lead at the trading post.

Dumont looked back over his shoulder and grinned when he saw Garth and McCready ushering Longarm and Melinda into the room. "Lookee here, Hair-Trigger," he crowed to Thompson, "we got us a good-lookin' gal to keep us company." He smiled at Melinda and asked, "You want to see my pecker?"

"Keep it in your pants and keep an eye on that blacksmith shop," Garth ordered. "There'll be time for pecker wavin' later, after we've killed those three varmints."

"I don't rightly see how we're gonna do that, Colonel," said Thompson. "They're holed up in there good and tight."

"Don't worry, Uncle Haygood and me are workin' on

a plan." Garth wagged the gun barrel at Longarm and Melinda. "You two sit down and put your hands behind your backs." He frowned. "What are we gonna use for rope to tie 'em up?"

"The marshal's shirt is already a mite torn up," McCready pointed out. "Rip some strips offa it."

"Yeah, that'll work."

Longarm sat there, disgusted, as yet another shirt was destroyed. This one was left in tatters around his muscular torso by the time Garth and McCready got through turning it into bonds to lash his wrists together, as well as Melinda's.

At least as they sat there leaning against the counter, they were able to rest their shoulders on each other. Longarm hadn't forgotten how Melinda had turned on him, but right now she was the closest thing he had to an ally in Abaddon.

"What are we going to do, Custis?" she whispered to him as the four outlaws huddled together to discuss their strategy. "We have to get out of this somehow."

"So you can steal your grandpa's loot for yourself?"

"Damn it, I have as much right to that money as anybody else!"

Longarm wasn't going to waste his breath arguing with her. If she hadn't been willing to resort to murder to get her hands on the loot, he might have been willing to go along with her claim, even though he didn't fully agree with it.

Of course, he didn't *know* that she would have killed him and McCready. That could have been a bluff. When the time came, she might not have been able to pull the trigger. The way things stood now, there was a good chance they would never know.

A particularly hard gust of wind rattled the walls of the trading post. The sand that was already inside blew across the floor, and more sand from outside sifted in through all the cracks. Melinda shivered as she leaned against Longarm.

"I hate the sound of that wind. It sounds like it's going to blow forever."

Longarm peered through the open doorway. The air was so thick with sand that it was getting harder to make out the buildings across the street.

Suddenly, Thompson said loudly, "I don't care if it is gettin' darker. I'm not goin' out there. Those bastards can still see me."

"Somebody's got to get to those wagons and find something that'll burn," argued Garth. "Otherwise, it's a standoff. None of us have food and water."

Thompson gestured toward Dumont. "Well, then, send Iron Mike out. He's littler than I am, so he'll be a smaller target."

Dumont cackled. "Not if they aim at my pecker. It's bigger'n anybody else's around here."

Longarm thought it was a wonder that none of the other outlaws had already shot Dumont for going on about his pecker. He had barely been around the man, and he was ready to blow a hole in him. For other reasons, too, of course, such as the fact that Dumont was a murderer and a thief—but shutting him up would be good, too.

McCready turned and jabbed a thumb in Longarm's direction. "Why don't we send ol' Marshal Long out to the wagons?" he suggested.

Garth snorted. "Have you gone loco, Uncle Haygood? There could be guns in those wagons."

"Yeah, but we'd have the gal, and the marshal'd be afraid to try to double-cross us as long as she's in danger."

"How do you know that? Didn't you say she was gonna kill both of you to get that loot for herself?"

McCready waved a gnarled hand. "Yeah, but that don't matter none. She's still a gal, and the marshal's one o' them there chivalrous fellers. He'll do what he can to protect her. That's just the way the Good Lord made him."

Longarm's jaw tightened. Unfortunately, McCready was right about that. He couldn't stand by and watch Melinda be hurt if there was anything he could do to prevent it.

"Anyway," McCready went on, "I got me an idea how we can keep the marshal from tryin' anything funny. He can't get a gun from the wagons if he ain't got no place to carry it."

Garth thought about that for a second and then started to nod. "Yeah, that might work," he said.

Melinda whispered, "What are they talking about, Custis?"

"I ain't quite sure," said Longarm, "but I got a hunch it ain't gonna be anything good."

While Dumont and Thompson continued to keep an eye on the blacksmith shop, Garth and McCready came over to the counter. Garth drew his gun and covered Longarm while he said, "Help him up, Uncle Haygood."

McCready helped Longarm to his feet. The big lawman asked, "Just what is it you fellas have in mind?"

"Why, it ain't nothin' such of a much," said McCready. "You're gonna go out to them wagons, Marshal, and rustle around amongst 'em until you find enough whiskey or coal oil or whatever to set that blacksmith shop on fire. You go start the blaze and then come back here."

"In other words, you want me to do your dirty work for you, and risk getting my ass shot off while I'm doing it."

"Well, it's funny you should put it that way . . .'cause you're a-gonna be doin' this without your clothes on."

Longarm couldn't stop himself from exclaiming, "What the hell are you talking about, old son?"

Garth said, "There might be some guns in those wagons, too, but if you're naked, you won't have any place to carry one. If you try, we'll see it. So all you can do is what we tell you to do." Garth moved his gun so that the muzzle was only inches from Melinda's face. She paled and gulped as she found herself staring down the Colt's barrel. "Unless you want this pretty little lady not to be so pretty anymore with her face blown off."

"Take it easy," said Longarm. "I didn't say I wouldn't cooperate."

"You'd damned well better, if you know what's good for the gal. Things can get mighty rough on her before we're through with her, you know."

McCready ripped what was left of Longarm's shirt off him, then knelt to pull off his boots. Longarm thought about kicking the old owlhoot in the head, but if he did that, Garth would probably just slam him with the butt of the pistol, and that wouldn't accomplish anything except to maybe get him a busted skull.

So he reined in the anger that he felt as McCready straightened and said to Garth, "I ain't takin' his pants off, Colonel. He'll have to handle that his ownself."

"All right," Garth nodded. "Untie him."

Longarm turned so that McCready could loosen the bonds on his wrists. When his hands were free again, he followed Garth's orders and took his trousers off.

"How about I leave the balbriggans on?" he asked.

Garth shook his head. "Nope. All of it comes off."

"Don't worry, Marshal," McCready said. "I don't reckon Miss Kelly's gonna see anything she ain't already seen before, now is she?"

Longarm didn't say anything in response to that gibe. He peeled the long underwear off and then stood there with his jaw set tightly.

"Here are some matches," said Garth as he handed over a little tin box of lucifers. "You can use those to start the fire. Once the blacksmith shop is burnin', just stay out of the way while we cut down those varmints as they come runnin' out."

Longarm bit back the angry words that wanted to come out of his mouth. He felt like telling Garth what he could do with those matches. Instead, he took the lucifers and said, "I'm goin' out the back. They'll be less likely to see me that way."

"Whatever you want to do," said Garth. "Just remember what's ridin' on you, Marshal." He ran the barrel of his gun along Melinda's cheek to reinforce his point. Longarm saw her trembling as the cold steel caressed her skin.

Longarm turned and stalked toward the rear of the trading post. McCready followed him, and when they reached the back door, the old-timer said quietly, "I wish things had worked out a mite different, Marshal. I surely do."

Longarm looked back at him. "If you want me to believe that, Haygood . . . you make sure nothing happens to that girl."

McCready shook his head. "I'm afraid that's in your hands now, Marshal."

Longarm stepped out into the growing sandstorm.

McCready pulled the door closed behind him. Instantly, Longarm felt a million tiny stings as the wind-borne particles of sand jabbed into his bare skin.

He should have asked for a bandana to help keep some of the sand out of his nose and mouth, he thought as he started making his way along the rear of the building. Garth probably would have refused, but it wouldn't have hurt anything to ask. Longarm cupped a hand over the lower half of his face instead and tried to breathe through it.

When he reached the corner, he turned and trotted past the well. The sand had drifted deeper around the wall but hadn't covered it yet. The way it was going, it would, though.

At the front corner of the building, he paused and edged his head around to have a look. He could still see the blacksmith shop sitting catty-corner across the street from the trading post, even though the air was thick with sand. As he watched, a spurt of gun flame came from the doorway of the shop as one of the men holed up inside sent a shot toward the trading post. Instantly, Dumont and Thompson responded with shots of their own. Longarm didn't figure anybody on either side was hit. As Garth had said, it was a standoff.

The three wagons were parked in a line in front of the trading post. The oxen had been taken up the street to a corral that had been formed by running rope between two of the buildings at both ends of the space between them.

Longarm darted to the back end of the wagon closest to him and climbed inside. He didn't know if the men inside the blacksmith shop had spotted him, but he didn't hear any shots. Even if they had seen him, they might not have believed their eyes. The sight of a big, naked man running around in a sandstorm would have anybody doubting his vision.

This was the wagon where Melinda had slept the night before, but it had several crates full of supplies in it. Longarm found what he was looking for right away. One of the crates had several bottles of whiskey in it. He took them out and pulled their corks with his teeth, then started looking for a knife.

He didn't find one, but he found a small hatchet instead and made do with that. He was able to cut several strips off the canvas cover over the back of the wagon. He twisted those strips into makeshift fuses and inserted them into the necks of two of the whiskey bottles so that they reached down into the liquor. Then he sat there counting to himself as he watched the brown whiskey slowly soak its way up the white canvas.

It took about ten minutes for the fuses to be saturated. Once he had determined that, Longarm cut more of the strips and wadded them into the necks of the remaining three bottles. He arranged them around a box he'd also found in the wagon and lit the fuses.

Then he picked up the first two bottles he had prepared and climbed quickly out the back of the wagon. Taking a deep breath, he ran across the street.

This time the men in the blacksmith shop spotted him, all right. They opened fire on him. Bullets kicked up sand around his feet. The outlaws in the trading post started shooting as well, but their slugs were directed toward the blacksmith shop and made the men there duck back into cover. That gave Longarm enough breathing room to reach the far side of the street, where the men in the blacksmith shop couldn't get an angle at him.

Hugging the buildings, he moved along the street until

he crouched at the corner of the blacksmith shop. The big open door was in the middle of the building. Longarm had to set the whiskey bottles down in order to strike a match. He turned his back to the wind, hunched over, and scratched one of the lucifers to life on the wall.

The wind blew it out before he could light the fuse in one of the whiskey bottle bombs.

Muttering in disgust, Longarm checked to see how many more matches he had. Only three, he saw. That could prove to be a problem. But he would have to do the best he could, because he'd gone too far to back out now. Across the street, those other canvas fuses were burning slowly up the sides of the bottles, toward the whiskey that was soaking into the canvas and creeping the other direction.

Longarm lit another match, grabbed one of the bottles, and jammed the flame against the liquor-soaked cloth. It caught instantly, flaring up in blue fire. Knowing he had only seconds to act, Longarm sprang into the street and flung the bottle as hard as he could at the open door. It sailed through even as the men holed up in there opened fire on him. He threw himself toward the alley beside the building again as bullets whipped past his head.

Somebody inside yelled, and then the bottle exploded. Longarm heard the blast, followed by a man's scream. He struck another match, lit the fuse on the second bomb, and rolled into the street. Bullets whined through the air above him as he pitched the bottle underhanded into the shop. Then he launched into another desperate roll, this time away from the searching lead.

The second bottle exploded in a ball of fire when it had barely cleared the doorway, sending splinters of glass spraying through the interior of the shop. Longarm lay on his belly, his whole body covered now with a thick coating of sand, and waited to see what was going to happen.

He didn't have to wait long, as smoke began to billow out of the shop. He heard a crackling sound and looked up. The wall next to him was on fire, flames spurting out from the cracks where it joined the roof. As old and dry as that wood was, the place would go up like a tinderbox.

Longarm scrambled to his feet. Black smoke was pouring out the open door now. Two men suddenly stumbled through the smoke, coughing violently as they fired toward the trading post across the street. A volley of shots rang out from O'Sullivan's place. The slugs ripped through the two men. They managed to stay on their feet for a second, but then they went down under the withering hail of lead. They lay on the sand, unmoving.

The third man had to still be inside the blacksmith shop. The smoke was so thick in there now, the flames so fierce, that Longarm didn't see how anyone could survive them. It was possible that the third man was dead to start with, killed by one of the exploding bottles.

Warily, Longarm moved out into the street. At the same time, Garth, Dumont, Thompson, and McCready emerged from the trading post, guns in their hands. "Stay away from them, Long!" cried Garth, and Longarm knew the outlaw meant the two men lying in front of the blacksmith shop. They had dropped their guns, and Garth didn't want Longarm getting his hands on them.

Longarm held up his hands to show Garth that he wasn't going to try anything. He didn't want Garth getting trigger-happy now. He estimated that about six minutes had passed since he'd lit the fuses on those other bottles.

Grinning, Garth came toward him. "Good job, Marshal," he said. "Of course, now that you've helped us take care of that little problem, you know we ain't got any reason to keep you alive."

He pointed his revolver at Longarm.

"Sorry, Marshal," said McCready. "Wish it could be some other way."

Garth glared over his shoulder at his uncle. "Don't apologize to this damned lawdog, Uncle Haygood. He's just gettin' what's comin' to him, the no-good son of a—"

Across the street, the three bottles of whiskey in the wagon exploded.

Flame shot out the openings at the front and back of the wagon, as well as a sheet of fire that rose up and engulfed the canvas cover itself. As if that wasn't enough, the cartridges in the box of ammunition around which Longarm had arranged the bottles began to detonate as well, creating a larger explosion and a huge racket. All four of the outlaws turned to stare.

Longarm dived forward, grabbed both of the revolvers that had been dropped by Barstow's men as they were gunned down, and came up shooting. He didn't know how many bullets he had left, but he didn't intend to waste any of them.

His first shot was aimed at Hair-Trigger Thompson's chest but broke Thompson's left shoulder instead when the outlaw shifted. The gun in Longarm's other hand belched fire as he snapped a shot at Dumont. Iron Mike went down hard. Longarm's third shot missed by a whisker and plucked the hat from Garth's head instead of boring through his brain the way Longarm intended. All in all, though, it wasn't bad shooting considering that Longarm was running as he fired and he couldn't see all that well because his eyes were full of sand and grit as the wind began to really howl.

He heard a couple of shots over the wind but didn't break stride as he sprinted toward the trading post. He vaulted onto the porch and ran inside, his bare feet slapping against the sand on the floor.

Melinda cowered against the counter. Whatever she'd been expecting to come through that door, it probably wasn't a naked, wild-eyed, deputy United States marshal with a gun in each hand. "Custis!" she cried.

He turned and saw a dark shape darting through the clouds of sand. He threw a shot at it, then pulled the trigger again only to have the hammer fall on an empty chamber. Tossing the empty Colt aside, he ran to Melinda and reached down to grab her by the arm and haul her to her feet.

"Come on," he said. "Let's get out of here."

"Wh-where are we going?"

"I don't know, but we can't defend this place." The trading post had too many doors, and he had only one gun now, with no telling how many bullets left in it. For all he knew, the Colt in his hand might be empty.

Without taking the time to untie Melinda's hands, he hustled her out the back door. If Garth and McCready were smart, they would have split up and circled the building. His eyes darted back and forth, but he didn't see anybody through the swirling sand.

The wind was getting so bad now that it was hard to see more than a few feet. He felt like the skin on his entire body had been scraped raw by the sand. If the storm got much worse, the few people left alive in Abaddon might have to hunker down and wait for it to blow over before they did anything else. McCready was no fool; he would know that running around the settlement in a blinding sandstorm like this was a good way to get lost and wind up wandering around the desert until you collapsed and the sand covered you like a grave.

Longarm and Melinda reached the end of the building. Longarm paused to risk a look around the corner. He didn't see anything except the wildly blowing sand. "Turn around," he told Melinda, and when she did so, he tugged the strips of torn shirt off her wrists, freeing her arms.

She threw her arms around him and huddled against him. "Custis, what are we going to do?" she asked over the shriek of the wind.

"We'll see if we can hide in one of these other buildings."

"Won't they look for us?"

"Maybe . . . maybe not. They're gonna have to get out of this storm, too."

He led her around the building next to the trading post, looking for a way in. That wasn't hard, because all the doors and windows were long gone. They climbed in through a window, and even though the wind still whipped through all the cracks and openings, it wasn't as fierce in there as it had been outside.

Melinda sank down on the sand-covered floor in exhaustion. "I wish I'd never even heard of Abaddon," she said.

"What about that buried treasure?" asked Longarm.

"The hell with the treasure! It's not worth dying over! It's not worth all the killing that's already gone on."

To Longarm's way of thinking, she should have considered that before she set out to find her grandfather's buried loot in the first place. Saying so wouldn't really accomplish anything, though, so he kept it to himself.

Instead, he took advantage of the chance to open the gun's cylinder and see how many rounds were left in it. He grunted.

"What?" asked Melinda.

"Two bullets left."

She laughed humorlessly. "One for each of us. Should I go first, Custis, or would you like to?"

Longarm snapped the Colt's cylinder closed, turned, and stalked over to her. He reached down to take hold of her arm and pull her to her feet.

"Nobody's taking that way out," he grated. "We're still alive, and that means we can still fight. We just got to figure out how."

Her chin jutted defiantly at him. "That's mighty bold talk for a naked man with a nearly empty gun." Suddenly, she reached down and took hold of his cock, which had started to get hard because he was close to her. "What about this gun, Custis? Is it nearly empty, too?"

The howling wind shook the building around them as Longarm growled in a voice husky with desire, "Why the hell don't we find out?"

Chapter 13

It was loco, of course. They had at least two men hunting them, wanting to kill them. But Melinda ripped off her already torn shirt while Longarm pushed her trousers down over her sleek hips. The room they were in had only one window and one interior door. Longarm figured he could keep an eye on them while he and Melinda were busy.

Anyway, with the odds against them, what the hell did it matter how they spent the next few minutes?

His shaft was fully erect by now. Melinda wrapped both hands around it and pumped as if she were trying to get him even harder. That wasn't going to happen, since he was already as hard as a rock, but Longarm didn't try to dissuade her from what she was doing. She leaned over and began licking it, then stopped and made a little spitting noise.

"Sorry," she said. "Sand. I swear, it gets in everywhere."

"Let's see about that," said Longarm as he sank to the floor and pulled her down with him.

She turned and lay atop him so that her face was nestled in his groin. Clasping his manhood, she began to lick it from base to crown. At the same time, her hips rested on his chest and her thighs straddled his head, so the fleshy folds of her sex were only inches from his mouth. He used his thumbs to part them and then closed that gap, spearing his tongue into her. That made her gasp with delight. He slid his middle finger into the puckered brown opening just above her sex, and that brought a low growl of passion from her.

She was right about the sand; it got in just about everywhere. But between his enthusiastic licking and her own juices, which were flowing freely now, most of it was soon washed away.

The arousal caused by Longarm's intimate caresses made Melinda's hips pump slowly. She fastened her lips around the head of his cock and sucked hard. At the same time, she cupped his balls and squeezed.

For several minutes, they tormented each other this way, then Melinda suddenly lifted her head. Longarm felt a pang of disappointment that the French lesson was over, but the disappointment was short-lived. Melinda twisted around on top of him and gasped, "I've got to have you inside me, Custis!"

She wasted no time in climbing on and impaling herself on his hard shaft. Nor was there anything slow and sensuous about their lovemaking. Melinda rode him hard, and Longarm drove up into her with swift, powerful thrusts. It was as if they were in a race to the finish line . . . which, in fact, they might well be.

This race was against death, though. They sought the culmination of their desire before their enemies found them.

Given that sense of urgency, it didn't take long before shudders started to ripple through Melinda's body. Longarm surged up into her and gave in to his own release, flooding her with his hot juices as she spasmed atop him.

Longarm was lost in the pleasure that cascaded through him as he clutched Melinda, but not so far gone that he didn't hear the sudden footstep at the door. With his left arm, he swept Melinda aside as he sat up and with his right hand plucked the gun from the floor beside him, where he had set it down when they started to make love.

As Melinda cried out in surprise, Iron Mike Dumont burst into the room, waving his gun from side to side as he searched for a target. Then his frantic gaze landed on Longarm and his eyes widened in surprise as they dropped to the big lawman's crotch.

"Holy shit!" he exclaimed. "It's bigger'n—"

That was as far as he got before the bullet from Longarm's gun smashed between his eyes and bored on through his head, exploding out the back in a pink, gray, and white spray of blood, brains, and bone.

Longarm was on his feet by the time Dumont's corpse hit the floor. He sprang across the room and grabbed the gun Dumont had dropped.

"Stay down," he called to Melinda as he put his back against the wall next to the door. After a moment, when it became obvious that no one else was about to rush into the room, he bent over and placed the gun he had just used to kill Dumont on the floor, then slid it across the room toward her. "There's only one bullet in it now, but it might come in handy."

He grabbed Dumont's shirt and dragged the little man's carcass out of the doorway into the other room. The loops on Dumont's shell belt were full of ammunition.

Longarm thumbed the cartridges out of the loops and checked the cylinder of Dumont's gun. It had three rounds in it, so Longarm filled the other three chambers. Then he tossed five more bullets across the room to Melinda and told her to reload the gun he had given her.

"Full wheel," he said. "Just be careful, because the hammer'll be resting on a live round."

She nodded as she slid the bullets into the Colt. "You know, Custis, I haven't really used a gun that much."

"That's a double-action revolver," he explained. "Point it and pull the trigger. Make sure you've got a good grip on it, though. It'll kick considerably harder than that pea-shooter you had this morning."

"That seems like a year ago," said Melinda with a weary sigh.

"Yeah, a heap's happened since then."

"Do you think the others heard that shot?"

"I don't know," said Longarm. "The way the wind's blowing, they might not have. They could be all the way at the other end of town, looking for us too. Or they might be hunkered down in the trading post, waiting for the storm to blow over before they come after us again."

He studied Dumont's body briefly and saw a blood-stain on the right side of the man's shirt. That had to be where he'd hit Dumont during that gunfight in the street. From the looks of it, the wound was only a deep crease, enough to knock the man down at the time but not bad enough to put him out of action for very long.

The sky was so full of dust that it began to look like twilight outside. Shadows gathered thickly inside the room where Longarm and Melinda waited. After a while, he told her, "Keep an eye on the door and the window as best you can."

"What are you going to do?"

Longarm knelt beside Dumont's corpse. "Thought I'd see if I can make this hombre's clothes fit me."

Melinda laughed and shook her head. "Sorry, Custis. You're twice his size. Everywhere, more than likely."

"Good thing ol' Iron Mike can't hear you say that. He'd be sorely disappointed."

Longarm pulled Dumont's trousers off and used the Barlow knife he found in one of the pockets to cut the legs off below the knees and then slit the sides of what was left. He took the pieces he had cut off and sliced them into strips that he tied together to use as a crude belt. He was able to get the trousers on and tie them into place with the belt, although the buttons on the fly didn't come anywhere close to fastening.

Melinda laughed again. "Custis, you look ridiculous."

"I ain't finished yet," Longarm told her. Dumont's gunbelt was big enough to fit around his waist. The little outlaw had worn it pulled up all the way. Longarm had to use the point of the knife to gouge out a new hole before he could fasten the buckle, but it worked and helped keep up the trousers.

Then he cut the sleeves off Dumont's bloodstained shirt and used the knife to enlarge the arm holes a little. After those modifications, he was able to wear it like a vest.

"I'm sorry," said Melinda, "I should have waited before I said anything."

"Don't look so ridiculous now, huh?"

"No, you still look utterly ridiculous," she said, "but I should have waited to get the full effect."

"It's better than running around naked."

Melinda looked down at her own nudity. "That reminds me . . ."

"Don't do anything about it on my account."

"You don't have places where the sand's trying to creep in again."

Longarm wasn't so sure about that, but he didn't argue with her as she began to pull her clothes back on. Her shirt was so tattered that it would barely tie together in the front, but she did the best she could with it.

He felt a little better now. He was dressed, sort of, and more importantly, they had a couple of guns and a decent number of bullets for those weapons, as well as the knife. The odds looked a whole heap better.

They couldn't fight that storm, though. The smart thing would be just to wait it out, unless Garth, McCready, and Thompson came looking for them.

Longarm sat down where he could watch the door and moved Melinda over so that she had a better view of the window. "We don't have any friends here," he told her, "so if you see anybody moving around out there, don't hesitate to pull the trigger."

"All right." She hesitated. "Custis, what are you going to do about me?"

"What do you mean?" he asked, even though he had a pretty good idea what she was talking about.

"I mean, assuming that we get out of this alive, are you going to arrest me?"

"What for? You hired those hombres to drive some wagons out here. That ain't a crime as far as I can tell."

"I pointed a gun at you and threatened to kill you. Twice."

Longarm chuckled. "You know how many folks have pointed guns at me and threatened to kill me since I started carrying a badge for Uncle Sam? More than I can remember, that's for damned sure. If I tried to arrest all of 'em who're still walking around, the jails'd be too full to put anybody else in there."

"So you're going to just forget about what happened?" she insisted.

He sighed. "Look, Melinda, I ain't all that fond of what you did, but I reckon you had your reasons. I ain't lived your life and don't know how you think. And right now I'm more worried about living through this mess we're in. We'll worry about what happens after that when the time comes. You can only eat an apple one bite at a time."

"I suppose you're right. I still wish I hadn't gotten you into this, though."

Longarm shrugged. "I wind up in trouble on a pretty regular basis. I ain't gonna lose any sleep over it."

He wished a few minutes later that he hadn't mentioned sleep. The dim light and the relentlessly howling wind combined to make his eyelids heavy. And when his eyes were closed, he thought, at least more sand couldn't get in them. He wasn't sure if his eyeballs would ever stop feeling gritty after this ordeal.

Thirst helped keep him awake, and so did hunger. He hadn't had anything to eat or drink since early that morning, and although he wasn't sure how much time had passed, he felt like it had to be late in the afternoon by now. He couldn't judge by the light, that was for sure. As it grew darker and darker, he began to worry that the sand would drift up and eventually cover the buildings of Abaddon again, as it had before. If that happened, sand would fill their sanctuary, and he and Melinda would be entombed here. It was a grisly thought, but it kept him from getting too drowsy.

When the voice from outside began to come faintly to

his ears, he didn't really notice it at first. He thought it was just something in the wind. Then he realized that he was hearing words. More than words, actually.

Someone was calling his name.

"Marshal! Marshal Long!"

Longarm sat up. He glanced across the room and saw that Melinda had dozed off. Her head drooped forward, the long dark hair falling around her face. Her hands held the gun loosely in her lap. Longarm wondered if he had gone to sleep, too, without being aware of it. Maybe he was dreaming now.

No, he was definitely awake. He heard the voice calling again, "Marshal Long! Marshal Long!"

The wind distorted things so much it was hard to be sure, but Longarm thought the voice belonged to Haygood McCready.

Longarm got to his feet and went to the window. Melinda must have heard him moving around, because she started awake, lifting the gun in her hand and saying, "What? What?"

"Take it easy," he said, making his voice sharp enough to cut through the fog in her brain. "Don't shoot, Melinda. It's only me."

"Custis?" She knuckled her eyes. "What's going on?"

"Somebody's out there." Longarm nodded toward the window. "I think it's McCready."

Melinda scrambled to her feet. "McCready? What does *he* want?"

"I got no idea," replied Longarm with a shake of his head. He motioned Melinda back as she came toward him. "Don't get too close to the window. Watch the door, too, in case he's trying to distract us while the other two come at us."

Actually, Longarm didn't know if Hair-Trigger Thompson was still alive. He knew his shot had hit the outlaw hard, and it was possible Thompson might have bled to death or passed out from the wound. But he and Melinda had to proceed as if the odds against them were still three to two, until they knew better.

Longarm crouched beside the window and took a careful look out. He still heard someone calling his name, and he was more convinced than ever that it was Haygood McCready. He couldn't see anything, though, except the blowing sand.

Then suddenly he caught a glimpse of a figure moving around out there. The sand swirled up, hid it from view, then the shape stumbled into sight again. It was McCready, all right. His hat was gone, and his right hand clutched his left upper arm where a crimson stain spread slowly under his fingers.

"Marshal!" McCready shouted again.

A gun roared somewhere nearby. McCready ducked and clawed out the holstered revolver on his hip. He snapped two shots in return. Longarm didn't know if McCready had seen the muzzle flash of the shot directed at him, or if he was just firing blindly.

"Haygood!" Longarm called.

McCready's head jerked around.

Melinda said, "Custis, what are you doing? He's one of them!"

"Looks like maybe thieves have fallen out," said Longarm. "I'm playing that hunch, anyway." He leaned from the window. "Haygood, over here!"

McCready broke into a shambling run toward the building. He pouched his iron and practically dived through the window. Longarm grabbed the old-timer's vest and helped haul him into the building.

McCready fell through the window and sprawled on the floor. Longarm reached down and plucked the gun from his holster, then stepped back and trained both weapons he held on McCready. McCready looked up at him and said, "I wouldn't blame you nary a bit if you was to blow my head off, Marshal, after the things I done. But I give you my word, I don't mean you or the lady no harm."

Longarm didn't take his eyes off McCready as he inclined his head toward the window and said, "What's going on out there?"

"Ol' Colonel, he's a-huntin' me. He's gone plumb loco and wants to kill me."

"Why would he do that?"

"Because I stood up to him and told him we ought to just let you and Miss Kelly go. I said we could take the wagons and them chests full o' loot and leave you here, and chances were you'd never get outta the desert alive."

Longarm grunted. "Mighty kind of you."

McCready sat up and put his good hand over the wound on his left arm again. "It's better'n killin' you flat-out, ain't it? That's what my nephew wants to do. He says he ain't leavin' this place until you and the gal are dead. He don't even want to take her with him no more. He's gone kill-crazy, I tell you. I think maybe it's that hellacious wind that's done it to him." The old-timer drew in a deep breath and let it out in a sigh. "Or maybe he was always that way. I pure-dee hate to say it about my sister's boy, but I reckon he was always a mite touched in the head."

"So what did he do, take a shot at you just because you spoke up for us?"

"That's damn sure what he done! Said that if I wasn't gonna help him get rid of you, I could go to hell . . . and he'd send me there!" McCready shook his head. "I reckon he got to thinkin', too, about how it'd be better to split that loot three ways instead of four." He looked at Iron Mike Dumont's scrawny, mostly naked body lying just outside the door in the building's other room. "We didn't know Dumont was dead."

"Yeah, it's just Garth and Thompson now," said Longarm. "How bad is Thompson's wound?"

"He lost a heap o' blood, but Colonel got it tied up and stopped the bleedin'. It's ol' Hair-Trigger's left shoulder that's busted, so he can still use a gun. He's half-drunk from a bottle we found in one o' them wagons you didn't burn up, and mad as an ol' wet hen about you shootin' him." McCready chuckled. "That was a pretty neat trick you pulled with the wagon, Marshal. I ain't sure how you done it, but I sure weren't expectin' it."

Longarm nodded toward McCready's injured arm. "Garth's shot wounded you?"

"This? Shoot, it's just a little bitty scratch. Nary a thing to worry about. Although I ain't got so much blood left in these ol' veins that I can spare a whole heap of it, I reckon. But I'm fine. Lit a shuck out o' that tradin' post—that's where we was holed up—and thought I'd try to find you. We made a pretty good team before, Marshal. I was hopin' maybe I could throw in with you again."

"But Garth came after you?"

"Him or Thompson or both of 'em, I don't rightly know which of 'em was shootin' at me. Feller can't hardly see his own hand in front of his face out there in that danged ol' sandstorm." McCready paused. "How about it, Marshal? The odds'd be in our favor if we was to join forces again, even if it was just a temporary truce."

"What about those chests full of loot?"

"What about 'em? I didn't steal that stuff in the first place, and I ain't got no claim on it."

"Might not stop you from trying to get your hands on it later," Longarm pointed out.

McCready shrugged. "I reckon I had that comin', considerin' how I lied to you earlier and how I'm a retired owlhoot and all. But all I can do is give you my word, Marshal. I want to get the three of us outta this damn desert alive. That's all I'm after."

Longarm thought about it for a minute, then nodded. "All right," he said. "We'll call a truce, Haygood."

"Mighty fine," said McCready as Longarm handed his gun back to him. He slid the revolver into leather and asked, "What's our plan?"

"Stay alive," Longarm said. "You don't know where Garth and Thompson are right now?"

The old-timer shook his head. "No idea. Maybe still out there wanderin' around in the storm lookin' for me, or maybe they've gone back to the tradin' post. Are we goin' after them?"

"I think we're better off staying right where we are. They can only come at us from two directions, and we can cover both of them. I'd rather wait until the storm's over to have a showdown."

"Could be days." McCready licked his lips. "We're liable to get mighty thirsty by then. They can get to the wagons, get water and whiskey and food."

He had a point, thought Longarm. Waiting could back-fire on them.

"Maybe what we need to do is get to those wagons ourselves. Then we'd have some supplies, too, and we can fort up in one of them. The sideboards are thick enough to stop a bullet."

"Now, that there is a good idea. And when the storm's over, you can stand up on the seat where they can see you."

Longarm frowned. "And be a target, you mean?"

McCready gave him a sly smile. "Naw. I mean they'll be so dang tickled by that getup you got on, I can ventilate 'em whilst they're busy laughin' and a-slappin' their legs."

Chapter 14

Once they had decided to move, there was no point in waiting. The three of them went out the front door of the building. Longarm nodded to McCready to go first. He didn't think the old-timer was planning a double cross, but it wouldn't hurt anything to have McCready where he could keep an eye on him, either. Melinda went next, and then Longarm stepped out into the street.

Even though the terrible wind screeched and whooped through all the cracks in the buildings, the structures did help to break some of its force. You didn't really realize just how much, though, until you stepped out into the full power of it, thought Longarm. The wind buffeted him like a giant fist and made him stagger to the side as he walked.

McCready and Melinda were affected the same way. Melinda weaved from side to side like an hombre on a three-day bender, evidently almost unable to stay on her feet. Longarm moved up beside her and clasped her arm with his left hand to steady her. He had the revolver clutched tightly in his right hand.

McCready led the way toward the wagons. They were

just dim shapes when they started, but as they drew closer, Longarm could make them out better. The third one had burned until all that was left was its metal frame, but the fire hadn't spread to the other two vehicles or any of the buildings.

McCready dropped into a crouch at the corner of the trading post. He motioned Longarm and Melinda up alongside him and leaned close to them so that they could hear him over the wind without him having to shout.

"Colonel and Thompson may be in the tradin' post watchin' those wagons," he said. "I'll go first and see if I draw their fire."

Longarm nodded. "We can't cover you from here. You'll be on your own."

"Shoot, I know that. But if I make it, then I can cover the two o' y'all."

He drew his gun and then sprang out into the open, dashing toward the wagons as fast as he could. He only had about twenty yards to cover.

But guns began to roar from the windows of the trading post before McCready was halfway to the wagons. Luckily for him, the sand swirling in the air made it hard to aim accurately. He triggered a couple of shots toward the trading post as he hurried toward the wagons.

Then McCready was past the burned-out wagon and reached the middle one. He jammed his gun in its holster and grabbed the tailgate so he could pull himself up and over. His right leg jerked as he did so, and Longarm knew he was hit. McCready didn't go down, though. He was able to pull himself up and scramble over the tailgate into the safety of the wagon bed. As long as he stayed low, the sideboards would protect him.

Longarm wasn't sure how badly the old-timer was

wounded, but after a moment McCready's face appeared at the back of the wagon. His mouth moved, but Longarm couldn't make out the words. He saw McCready waving them on, though, and then McCready's gun began to blast as he pulled up the canvas cover on the side of the wagon and fired toward the trading post.

"Go!" Longarm told Melinda. "I'll be right behind you!"

Melinda dashed toward the wagons with Longarm following her. McCready's shots must have made Garth and Thompson duck for cover, because for a few seconds nobody shot at them as they ran.

But then flame spurted out one of the windows and a bullet whined off the metal frame of the burned-out wagon just as Melinda ran past it. She let out an involuntary cry of fright but didn't slow down. McCready dropped the tailgate as she approached, and she leaped into the wagon bed, sprawling on the bottom of it.

Longarm triggered a shot at the window where he had seen the muzzle flash, then he was at the middle wagon, too. He jumped, got a hand on the tailgate, and vaulted inside, rolling over as he landed so that he wound up on his belly.

McCready was still taking potshots at the trading post. Longarm joined him while Melinda lay behind them, catching her breath.

Longarm turned his head to look over his shoulder. The wagon had several crates full of supplies in it. They would have to keep their heads down, but they wouldn't starve.

"Go through those boxes and see if you can find any canteens," Longarm told Melinda.

McCready said, "I already seen somethin' even better amongst them supplies . . . canned peaches!"

Longarm grinned. A man could live on peaches, and the juice they were canned in, for a few days if he had to. Sooner or later, such a diet would play hell with a fella's digestion, but Longarm didn't figure they would be here long enough to have to worry about that.

He handed his knife to Melinda. "Open a few cans of those peaches," he said. "I reckon they'll taste mighty good right about now."

McCready's gun roared as he took another shot at the trading post. "Damn right."

The wagon shook a little under the force of the wind. The canvas cover billowed on the metal arches it was attached to. Longarm didn't figure the canvas would stay on there through the storm unless the wind died down soon. It was already tearing loose in places and starting to flap. If it came off and flew away, he and his companions would be more exposed to the storm, but the sideboards would still offer them some protection from the wind as well as from bullets.

At least they had food and drink here, and as he glanced around, Longarm spotted another box of .45 rounds. Barstow had brought along plenty of ammunition. Longarm wondered if the wagon master had been planning on double-crossing Melinda all along, even when he didn't know exactly what it was they were going after in the desert.

Melinda pressed a can of peaches into his hand. She had cut the top out with the knife. Carefully, so he wouldn't slice his lips on the sharp metal edges, Longarm brought the can to his mouth and drank deeply of the juice, draining just about all of it and not swallowing too much sand in the process. Then he stuck his fingers into the can, brought out a peach half, and popped it into his mouth. It tasted as good as anything he had eaten in a long, long time, and the juice was better than the finest whiskey.

Melinda opened one of the cans for McCready, too, and then one for herself. McCready let out a long sigh of satisfaction when he was finished with his.

"Almost makes gettin' shot again worth it," he said.

"How bad were you hit?" asked Longarm.

"Knocked a hunk o' meat outta my leg, that's all. I wouldn't want to have to ride twenty miles on that ol' mule o' mine right now, but I reckon I'll be all right." McCready shook his head. "Poor ol' mule. Reckon that first storm must've got her."

"Maybe she lived through it," said Melinda. "Maybe you can look for her when this is all over."

"Yes'm, I'll do that. Happen I'm still alive my ownself, that is."

Suddenly, with a ripping sound, the canvas cover tore loose even more. It was now fastened to the wagon's framework in only a couple of places. In the grip of the wind, it waved and fluttered and popped wildly.

"Hand me that knife," Longarm told Melinda. He took it from her and reached up to slash through the canvas where it was still attached. As soon as it came loose, the cover seemed to leap straight up into the air. It sailed away and was lost to sight in the blink of an eye.

"It's gettin' late," said McCready. "Gonna be dark soon. I don't reckon those ol' boys are gonna wait. They won't want us slippin' up on 'em in the dark."

"You're saying they'll make a run at us," Longarm said.

"I figure there's a mighty good chance of it. If they can get rid of us, they can unload the rest o' these supplies, carry 'em into the tradin' post, and wait out the storm there just as snug as any bug in a rug. When it's over, they'll get them treasure chests and load 'em up, probably head for Mexico. But ol' Colonel, he's smart enough to know he'll have to kill us first."

Longarm nodded. "Then it won't be long now. Melinda, you keep your head down when they charge us."

"The hell with that!" she said. "Point the gun and pull the trigger, you told me. I can do that."

Longarm grinned. "All right. But try to stay low as you can while you're doing it, and whatever you do, be careful not to shoot Haygood or me."

She snorted as if to say what she thought of that.

Longarm suddenly heard another noise over the howling and roaring of the wind. He turned his head and saw the roof being ripped off one of the other buildings. The wind had finally gotten to be too much for the nails holding the structure together. With a splintering racket, the roof came apart, and boards flew through the air.

"Get down!" Longarm cried. Those boards turned into deadly missiles in the grip of the wind. He and Melinda and McCready all ducked as debris pelted the wagon.

That distraction might have given Garth and Thompson the opportunity they needed to launch their attack, Longarm realized. Risking decapitation, he lifted his head and spotted dark shapes weaving through the sand toward the wagon from different directions. The outlaws had them trapped in a cross fire.

"Haygood!" he shouted. "Here they come!"

Colt flame spurted through the blinding sand. Longarm came up on one knee and returned the fire, aiming at the man to the rear of the wagon, while McCready rolled to the front end and began blazing away in that direction.

The boards weren't flying through the air anymore, but Longarm saw that without their extra support, the building that had lost its roof was collapsing. The other buildings were swaying in the terrible wind, too, except for the burned-out blacksmith shop and the sturdier trading post. Longarm wasn't sure even the trading post would survive this blow, though.

That thought flashed through his head, and it was all he had time for because he was too busy trading shots with Colonel Thaddeus Henshaw Garth. The outlaw was close enough for Longarm to recognize him now. Splinters flew from the top of the wagon side next to Longarm as one of Garth's bullets struck it. That was pretty good shooting, considering that with the wind and the flying sand, they were all firing almost blind.

"Get ready, Melinda!" he called to her, then rolled off the tailgate. "Now!"

Both of them opened fire again as Longarm hit the ground. Garth had made it to within ten feet of the back of the wagon. He stopped and rocked backward as the slugs fired by Longarm and Melinda pounded into his body. He managed to squeeze off a final shot, but his arm had already sagged and the bullet went harmlessly into the sand at his feet. Longarm triggered another round. This one went through Garth's beard and caught him in the throat, angling upward through his brain as blood spurted from severed arteries in a crimson fountain. The burly outlaw toppled over backward, landed with arms and legs splayed out, and didn't move again.

Longarm scrambled to his feet and turned to see how McCready was managing with Thompson. He was in time to see Thompson fall as McCready blasted another slug

through him. McCready was hunched over at the front of
the wagon bed, though, as if in pain.

"Haygood!" Longarm yelled as he ran to the front of
the wagon. He glanced at Melinda and saw that she was
pale and shaken but seemed to be all right otherwise.

McCready's gun slipped from his fingers as he pressed
his other hand to his midsection. Longarm circled the
wagon and caught hold of the old-timer's arm. "Are you
hit again?"

McCready looked up at him and said, "It ain't nary a
thing . . ."

Then his eyes rolled up in his head and he slumped to
the side.

Longarm slid his arms around McCready and lifted
him out of the wagon. "We have to get him inside!" he
called to Melinda. He started toward the trading post, but
before he could get there, one of the beams holding up the
porch roof broke with a loud crack. The roof started to
sag. Another beam snapped.

"Look out, Custis!" Melinda screamed behind him.

He saw what she meant. The roof was coming off the
trading post, too. The wind was too much. The whole
place might come down, and if they were inside it, they
would be crushed.

But they had to find some shelter somewhere.

An idea occurred to Longarm. He placed McCready on
the ground under the first wagon in line and then ran
down the street toward the makeshift corral where the
oxen had been penned up. He didn't know if any of the
beasts were still there, but luck was with him. The stolid
creatures were in the corral, seemingly unfazed by the
terrible sandstorm. Coughing as he breathed in just about
as much sand as air, Longarm cut the rope that ran be-

tween two of the swaying buildings and tied it to the harness of one of the oxen.

He led the ox back down the street. Melinda saw him coming and called, "What are you going to do with that thing?"

Longarm didn't take the time to answer. He told Melinda, "Get out of the wagon!" and then tied the rope to the middle arch that had held up the canvas cover over the back. Then he began slapping the ox on the rump and shouting at it.

The ox was slow to get the idea, but Longarm had spent a short period of time working as a bullwhacker when he was younger, so after a few minutes he was able to get the beast to pull. The wagon tilted and then went over, crashing onto its side. Longarm kept the ox moving until it had pulled the wagon around so that it was broadside to the wind. Then he untied the rope and let the ox go free.

"Get behind the wagon!" he told Melinda. It leaned at an angle, but the metal arches, although they bent a little, kept it from turning over completely. That formed a little niche that was out of the wind. Longarm picked up McCready and carried him over there. They crowded into the protected space with Melinda.

"Is this safe, Custis?" she shouted.

"As safe as anywhere we're gonna find in Abaddon!" The roof was mostly gone from the trading post now, and the other buildings were flying apart. The storm a couple of days earlier had been bad, but this one was a monster that threatened to scour the earth clean.

Longarm felt McCready stir as they huddled there, and as he looked down, the old-timer's eyes fluttered open. "Reckon the . . . jig's up . . . ain't it?" asked McCready.

"Don't give up yet," Longarm told him. "When this storm blows over, we'll get you some help."

"There ain't no . . . help to get . . . and this storm . . . ain't gonna blow over . . . This is . . . the end of the world . . . Marshal."

It sure as hell seemed like it, thought Longarm. After the Great Flood, the Good Lord had promised Noah that the world wouldn't end that way and had hung a rainbow in the heavens to seal the pledge.

But *El Señor Dios* hadn't said anything about sand, leastways not that Longarm could recall from the days when his ma still read the Scriptures to him. So maybe McCready was right. Maybe this really was the end of the world.

He pillowed McCready's head on his thigh, put his arm around Melinda's shoulders and pulled her tight against him, and then hunkered down to wait and see.

Chapter 15

The first thing that struck Longarm was how *quiet* it was. The wind had blown so hard, for so long, that at first he thought he had just gotten used to it and didn't hear it anymore. Even when there hadn't been any storms, the wind had still blown enough so that he could hear it sighing over the desert most of the time.

But now there was nothing. Utter stillness.

Except, he realized, for the soft, regular sound of Melinda Kelly's breathing as she lay in his arms.

Longarm didn't remember going to sleep. Just like during the first storm, he had drifted off into a stupor that had deepened into actual slumber sometime during the night. Now the light that struck his closed eyes told him it was morning. Squinting, he pried his eyelids open.

Nothing met his gaze except sand, as far as the eye could see.

Longarm lifted his head and gave it a little shake to clear away some of the cobwebs. He spat sand out of his mouth. His nose and eyes were clogged with it, too. Carefully, so as not to disturb Melinda, he slid his arm from around her and then pawed at his nose and eyes, clearing away as much of the grit as he could.

She stirred beside him, despite his efforts not to wake her, and murmured, "Custis?"

"Right here," he told her.

She lifted her head and rubbed at her own eyes until she could see him. "Where are we? What happened?"

Longarm looked up at the wagon leaning over them. The sand had drifted around the overturned vehicle and mounded up in front of it, but it hadn't risen high enough to close off the opening entirely. That was the reason they were still alive. Longarm reached out and shoved some of the sand aside, widening the opening so that they could crawl out of the little cave-like area that had formed.

"Looks like it's morning," he said. "The storm's moved on. It's mighty quiet now."

"Custis . . . where's Mr. McCready?"

Longarm had already realized that McCready was gone. The old outlaw had still been alive, although unconscious, when Longarm's awareness faded. Sometime during the night, McCready must have come to and crawled out into the storm for some reason. He was probably out of his head, thought Longarm. All he knew for sure was that McCready had left long enough ago so that all signs of his leaving had been erased by the wind.

"Reckon he lit a shuck out of here."

"But why? He couldn't have survived in that storm!"

"No," said Longarm, "it sure don't seem likely, does it? Especially as bad as he was hurt." He spat out some more sand. "We'd better take a look around and figure out what we need to do next."

He went first, crawling out from under the wagon.
What he saw as he stood up and surveyed their surroundings shocked him.

Or rather, what he *didn't* see.

Abaddon was gone.

All the buildings had collapsed, broken apart, been carried off by the wind. That was all he could figure. He saw
a few humps in the sand that might have been covered-over debris—or the bodies of dead outlaws. The other
wagon was gone as well. He wondered if the canvas cover
had acted like a sail, finally catching enough wind so that
the wagon rose and was carried off like a ship sailing
through a sea of sand.

"Oh, my God!" Melinda cried as she crawled out and
looked around. "What are we going to *do*?"

"First thing, we ain't gonna panic. Let's look around
and see what we've got to work with."

"Work with?" repeated Melinda. "We don't have *anything* to work with! There's nothing out here!"

"You're wrong about that," said Longarm. "We're out
here. And we can still think."

He had a pretty good idea where everything had spilled
out of the wagon when he used the ox to pull it over on its
side. He went to his knees and started digging in the sand.
A few minutes later, his fingers touched something.
Quickly, he cleared the sand away from it and came up
with a can of peaches.

Melinda gasped when she saw it, fell to her knees beside Longarm, and started digging, too. A half hour later,
they had a dozen intact cans of peaches.

The knife was still in the pocket of the trousers of Iron
Mike Dumont's that Longarm wore. He dug it out, opened

one of the cans, and he and Melinda split it. That eased the terrible hunger and thirst that had gripped them and made it a little easier to think.

"Those oxen wandered off during the storm," Longarm said, "but I'll bet they didn't go far. If I can find a couple of them and drive them back here, we can use them to set this wagon up, hitch 'em to it, and drive back to Brimstone."

Eager hope leaped to life in Melinda's eyes. "Do you really think we can do that?"

"I don't see why not, as long as I can find some of those critters. I'll start looking."

"What do you want me to do?"

"Stay here," Longarm told her. "I think I can find my way back all right, but if I happen to get lost, I'll fire three shots in the air. It'll be your job to answer with three shots of your own. Then I can follow the sound back to you."

She nodded. "All right." She stepped closer to him and threw her arms around him in a hard hug. "Good luck, Custis," she whispered.

Longarm stroked her hair with one hand and patted her back encouragingly with the other. Then he put a finger under her chin, tipped her head back, and kissed her. Their lips were dry and cracked, but the kiss was a good one anyway.

Any tracks left by the oxen as they wandered off had long since been erased by the storm, so all he could do was pick a direction and trudge off that way. The storm had come out of the east this time, so he figured the oxen would have put their rumps to the wind and headed west. Longarm walked that direction, feeling the heat of the sun on his back increase as the bright yellow orb rose higher in the clear blue sky.

Within a few minutes, he was out of sight of Melinda and the wagon. He kept walking as straight as he could, up and down the dunes, turning his head constantly so that his eyes could scan the desert in all directions for the missing oxen.

An hour later, he was about to give up when he suddenly spotted a dark shape against the sand, off to his left. As he turned and trotted in that direction, he saw another one nearby. His heart leaped in his chest when he came close enough to recognize two of the oxen just standing there dumbly. They might do so until they dropped dead of thirst, although chances were that when they got dry enough, they would start looking for water.

Longarm circled them and approached from the west. He yelled, slapped their rumps, and prodded them with the knife. Finally, he got them turned around and started toward the place where he'd left Melinda. Since the air was so still this morning, the marks he had left in the sand were visible, so he had no trouble backtracking himself. The worst part was the hot, bright sun.

The oxen stopped every so often and had to be hoorawed into moving again. Even when they were moving, they didn't go very fast. So it was almost midday by the time Longarm got back to the wagon with them. Melinda saw them coming from quite a ways off, he supposed. She ran to meet them when they were still a couple of hundred yards away.

"Custis, you found them!" she cried. "You found them!" She threw her arms around him again.

"Yeah, I was lucky, all right. Let's see if we can get the wagon back on its wheels without breaking an axle."

"Before you do that, I was looking around, and I found a water barrel that was on one of the wagons. It was mostly buried, but I dug out the top and there's still water in it."

Longarm grinned. "Good work! That'll sure make those oxen happier."

While the oxen were drinking from the partially buried water barrel, Longarm and Melinda cleared away as much of the sand from around the vehicle as they could, then cut up what was left of Dumont's shirt and made a couple of short lengths of rope out of it. Longarm was bare to the waist again. He had never had so much trouble keeping a shirt on, he reflected. By the time they got back to Brimstone, he was going to be blistered good and proper, but that was a small price to pay for their lives.

He tied the makeshift ropes from the oxen's harness to the wagon frame and prodded them into motion again. The axles creaked dangerously as the wagon began to shift, but it fell over onto its wheels before either axle could snap. The framework over the wagon bed was bent out of shape, but that didn't matter. The vehicle's wheels would still roll, and that was all that was important.

Longarm hitched the oxen to the wagon and rigged reins using the twisted and tied lengths of cut-up shirt. They finished digging out the water barrel and put it in the back. Melinda put the canned peaches in the wagon as well, except for one can that they split between themselves, like they had earlier.

As she was licking the last of the juice off her fingers, she said, "Custis . . . while you were gone, I looked for those chests."

Longarm hadn't even thought about the loot William O'Sullivan had buried here. He frowned and asked, "Did you find them?"

Melinda shook her head. "I can see where the well is. It's completely covered with sand and plugged up, the way it was before, but I'm pretty sure it's that hump right over there. So I walked north from it, and I found the place where the chests should have been, but they're gone."

"That ain't possible," said Longarm. "They're just covered up again, like everything else around here."

"But I dug down into the sand everywhere around there, and I didn't find them. They're just not there."

Longarm didn't believe that. The chests had been too heavy and low to the ground to blow away. The sand had drifted around them and buried them. He was sure of it. Melinda had just been mistaken in her calculation of where they were.

"I guess if you want to put together another outfit and come back out here later to look for them, I can't stop you," he said. "If it was me, though, after everything that's happened . . . I think I'd just leave 'em wherever they are."

She looked at him for a long moment, then sighed and nodded. "I suppose you're right. Like I said . . . what's in those chests isn't worth all the killing."

"That's right." Longarm drew her into his arms and kissed her again, then said, "Now, let's get the hell out of here."

Longarm let out a sigh as he settled back in the big galvanized tub and the water sloshed around him. This was the third bath he had taken since getting back to Brimstone earlier this evening. He had kept the folks who worked in the hotel busy dumping and hauling water. Now, though, he finally felt like he had gotten all the sand off him.

Melinda sighed, too, as she snuggled back against him and his arms tightened around her nude form. She had joined him for this bath, after taking a couple of her own. She rested her head on his shoulder and said, "It all seems like a dream now, Custis."

"More like a nightmare," said Longarm.

"Yes. A nightmare. That's why, after tonight, I'm never going to think about it again. I'm going to San Antonio, and I'm going to find a job, a real job, and start a new life. An honest life."

"That sounds like a mighty fine plan." Longarm wasn't sure if he believed her or not. He figured she meant what she said . . . right now. Whether she could stick to it, well, that would be up to her. He had to get back to Denver. He was sure that Billy Vail had another job waiting for him by now.

He just hoped that it didn't involve sand.

Melinda was sitting on his lap. Having a wet, naked, beautiful young woman in his arms meant that his cock was hard, of course. Melinda had her legs parted a little so that his shaft was nestled between her inner thighs, resting against the soft folds of her core. The head of it poked up above the triangle of dark hair where her thighs came together.

She glanced down at it and laughed. "Look, Custis. It looks like I have a, ah, male member, too."

"Well, we'd best do something about that." Longarm shifted his grip on her and lifted her a little in the water. When he set her back down, it was on his manhood, which slid easily into her.

Melinda gasped in pleasure. "My God, Custis, that feels so good," she breathed. "I'm so full of you . . ."

This time they could take it slow and easy. They sort of had to, since both of them were sunburned and too much frolicking around would be painful. Long, languorous minutes passed, and when their culmination finally washed over them, it was a slow, sensuous eruption that left them both drained.

They were lazing there in the tub, eyes closed, when the door of the hotel room burst open and a man with a hideously burned and disfigured face rushed in, yelling curses and brandishing a shotgun. Longarm barely had time to recognize the intruder as Barstow before the double barrels of the Greener swung toward them.

Longarm snapped up the Colt he'd left on a chair right beside the tub and fired just before Barstow could pull the shotgun's triggers. The .45 slug smashed into Barstow's chest and drove him backward. His finger jerked on the shotgun triggers, but the twin barrels were pointed upward as Barstow fell, so the double load of buckshot blew a huge hole in the ceiling, instead of in Longarm and Melinda. Barstow flopped on his back in the corridor and didn't move again. Down the hall somewhere, a woman started to scream, probably because she had peeked out the door of her room and seen the bloody corpse lying there.

Melinda hadn't even had time to cry out. Now, as the echoes of the shotgun blast died away, she said, "Custis . . . was that . . . ?"

"Barstow? Yeah. I reckon he was the third man in that blacksmith shop. He must've kicked his way out the back wall while it was on fire. Burned him pretty bad but didn't kill him. No telling how he got back here. Maybe he walked all the way. Hate will drive a man when nothing else will."

Melinda shuddered. Longarm's left arm was still around her and drew her closer. "My God," she whispered. "Will this nightmare ever be over?"

"It's over," Longarm said confidently. "It's over."

Three days later, he was in El Paso, waiting to catch a train back to Denver. He and Melinda had taken the stagecoach from Brimstone to San Antonio, and they had said their bittersweet farewells there. Then he'd caught a Southern Pacific train to El Paso, where he would switch to the Denver & Rio Grande for the rest of the trip back to Colorado.

He was sitting in the depot wearing a brown tweed suit and a new snuff-brown Stetson, with a folded newspaper in his lap. He took a cheroot from his vest pocket, snapped a lucifer to life with his thumbnail, and set fire to the gasper. Life was good.

Then, as he glanced idly through the open door of the station, he saw a man walking along the street, and something about the slightly bow-legged figure struck Longarm as familiar. The man wore fancy duds, but he walked like an old cowboy—or an old outlaw—and when he turned to cross the street, Longarm caught a glimpse of an angular, beard-stubbled face. Then the man moved on, out of sight.

Longarm took a deep breath. Suppose Haygood McCready hadn't been as badly wounded as he'd thought. And suppose that other wagon *hadn't* been carried off by the storm. Longarm had rounded up a couple of the missing oxen. McCready could have done the same thing. Sometime during the night, he could have hitched up the wagon, loaded those chests full of O'Sullivan's loot, and driven off into the storm . . .

"That's the most loco notion I've ever heard in my life," he said out loud as he took the cheroot from his mouth. Haygood McCready was somewhere out there in the desert, his body covered for all time by the sand.

And yet Longarm knew he could never prove that.

A man sitting farther down the bench turned and asked, "Did you say something to me, friend?"

"Nope," said Longarm. He clamped his teeth on the cheroot again and lifted the newspaper, opening it to help him pass the time until the train arrived. "Nary a thing."

Watch for

LONGARM AND THE SKULL MOUNTAIN GOLD

the 375th novel in the exciting LONGARM
series from Jove

Coming in February!

GIANT-SIZED ADVENTURE FROM
AVENGING ANGEL LONGARM.

BY TABOR EVANS

2006 Giant Edition:

LONGARM AND THE
OUTLAW EMPRESS

2007 Giant Edition:

LONGARM AND THE
GOLDEN EAGLE SHOOT-OUT

2008 Giant Edition:

LONGARM AND THE
VALLEY OF SKULLS

2009 Giant Edition:

LONGARM AND THE
LONE STAR TRACKDOWN

penguin.com/actionwesterns

M456AS0409

DON'T MISS A YEAR OF

Slocum Giant
by
Jake Logan

Slocum Giant 2004:
Slocum in the Secret Service

Slocum Giant 2005:
Slocum and the Larcenous Lady

Slocum Giant 2006:
Slocum and the Hanging Horse

Slocum Giant 2007:
Slocum and the Celestial Bones

Slocum Giant 2008:
Slocum and the Town Killers

Slocum Giant 2009:
Slocum's Great Race